The Genetic Scanner

Revision 3.0

THIS BOOK BELONGS TO

_____

Perché per sentirsi bene, bisogna star bene, mentre per sentirsi amati, qualcun altro deve volerci bene? — John Little Horn

Why to feel good, you feel good, to feel loved, someone else must take well? - John Little Horn

The Genetic Scanner — Revision 3.0

Written by Giovanni Correddu under the pseudonym John Little Horn between 2007 and 2010

Englilsh edition

Printed from:

Lulu

www.lulu.com/corgiov

INDICE

Chapter I

Good morning. I hope that you don't want to skip these introductory pages.

I am a humble human being, sickly for several years now; they still struggle to understand how he arrived at this point. Last night I dreamed a dream that told me a lot of "why", but many others are still there, in my mind, and I don't know if there will ever be an answer to them.

I could tell you directly my dream, but that there would be several questions, which I cannot answer. For this, it takes the beautiful Dr. Mary Ivanovo (Иванов Мариа). Ask her, and will respond with masterfully scientific sentences. Things that I couldn't even dream (and as I did last night, which is what requires explanation!).

By the way, I speak, I speak, and still speak, and you do not know my name! That rude! It is better than I do forgive. My name is Joann Rajok (Иоанн Рожок). You know, there is a legend about my last name. It states that my ancestors possessed a rhino horn, in which she did grow a plant. Thus, he was nicknamed Rog (Рог). "Rog" in Russian means "horn". His descendants were therefore called "Cornett", i.e. "Rajok". I don't know if this story is true, but I definitely wouldn't mind going back four centuries and make the acquaintance of this my ancestor. The dearest Dr. Mary would tell you: "Travel in time? You don't need. We already have a genetic code stored in our DNA, which tells the entire genealogy of the family of every individual". How I managed to say such a thing? I don't understand anything about Science! Do You See? The dream last night managed to stir something in me. What if...? Eh, no! They don't tell you all now, or you will ruin the beauty of reading my report on recent times (although I doubt that they will have to call it that, in fact, when you meet my friend of chapter III, you will understand better. Wait, don't go now, I got tell you something and then there's the chapter two!).

I know: you're curious about why I am so sickly, and well know my nationality. For one thing, it can be done, for the second, me and my friends we decided not to reveal our or our nationality (at least for now). We have very dangerous enemies, which might find themselves in his hands this book, and I don't want to risk that know details new! Don't ask me why extra things. As you read, there will be sufficient.

Now, instead, I'll let you get bored, explaining why they are so sickly. I was a healthy child, when I was born (Yes, I too have had the privilege of being born, you thought you could, right?). Yes, I was born, and I was a very beautiful baby. My mom always told me: when I saw for the first time, already seemed larger than the other kids my age. Should I show off? Perhaps, yes, given that over the years I've become sickly.

Then, a beautiful morning, when I was six, I was home alone, in the company of my childhood buddies, Alexei (Алекс) and Frederique was nine. In the backyard, they spoke of more and less — often taking me around— and me I pedaled like a madman. So it was that caught the flight. A bad maneuver made me kiss the tarmac: nose and Chin destroyed! I would have preferred Dr. Mary instead of asphalt, but we cannot do anything, now, especially after last night. But let's go back to that morning of twenty-one years ago. I still remember that my two friends rushed, but Alexei arrived quickly to my rescue, while Frederique went to call his father, why were rescue. I brought in a room in the back room of his father by Frederique. Alexei, seeing me cry, chased by an unbearable pain, began to make the faces. I between myself I thought: That's stupid! Don't you realize that I've become big? I was six years old, and in a few months will go to first grade!' I smile the same, so as not to offend him. To see him smile, I thought: 'When I will be better, and the blood will stop flowing, he will explain that those faces were not laugh I miss a bit. In that, Frederique said No! Don't laugh, or dies from loss of blood! Must keep my mouth still. You don't see that that's where he's done wrong?' 'Well said, Frederique! So do you!' I continued to think of me. Finally arrived my mom who told me: "I am away a few minutes, and I should not worry. My son! I'm glad you saved! I could get lost!" Eh, no! I was there, alive and well. Not enough a shot like that to destroy me, although, in fact, was that shot to change my life forever.

It took three years because I understood that my way of reacting had not my strong psyche, but a genetic change caused me the shot. I never said! Indeed, I would have never thought to know say so well! Last night has caused me another shot.

When I was almost ten years, I began to suffer from a chronic cold. Didn't understand why, whatever the season, seemed to always cooled, affected. A little time, and I realized that they are very allergic to sunlight. I couldn't stay in direct contact of the Sun: I formed first sunspot on the body, then they become bubbles — and restricting type hives — and finally the itching drove me crazy. I must say one thing: I can't remember a single occasion since I was born, where I suffered the cold. According to my dear Doctor, I have always had the DNA arranged for this genetic change. Already I do not understand what I write, then understand how it happened, it's even more complicated for my mind.

The fact is that one fine day; I discovered that this allergy, cold, could become a weapon of defense for the weakest. Yes, being in direct contact of the Sun, I realized that I became heavier. Someone called me brother red Incredible Hulk, but don't worry, I was pretty far from being his brother. I was raised as an only child! Anyway, I became Red, approached a piece of cloth to nose, and landed a deadly liquid: actually, I never killed anyone, but with this I can freeze the liquid.

Now I can finally tell you my real name, that of battle: Heart-Sun. Yes, forget my native identity, and learned that my real name, Heart-Sun. From now on, this will be the name that you will read and you will learn to love (especially if you're some nice readers).

The next chapter has been written by the most beautiful female doctor that I hadn't ever met. Soon I will therefore speak. But first let me explain how we met.

I was twenty-four. It was a hot summer day. My whole body was wet, and still did not know that it possesses the power of Heart-Sun. Still I did call Joann. I met this wonderful woman, and from that day you opened a friendship that connects like no other pair of friends may be linked. I still remember that I was waiting for the *automobile omnibus* back home (you wonder who has written? Bus!). The beautiful young woman was waiting. She too had twenty-four. I wanted to flirt with her, but I didn't know how to open the dialogue. I saw that he had a book in his hand, and asked: "What is it?"

"Is a book I'm studying for my master's thesis?"

"Nice!"

"The book or the fact that I am preparing a thesis?"

Subheading said: "Really, I wanted to say 'beautiful'".

"Can you repeat that? I did not understand".

"No, I said, nice that studies and interest you ... do not see well the title of the book".

"Genetics for everyone — New and old theories: a journey through time and into the human body".

"That title! Cringe!"

"There had never considered. You seem very clever, to arrive so quickly to conclusions". Yes, we were just made for each other, kindred spirits, we understand in a heartbeat!

"Thanks, but I don't understand anything about science, genetics, and these things here. Tell me, if you are preparing a thesis, perhaps you're also working on some project ... scientific?"

"Yes, I'm working on a new way to interpret and manipulate DNA".

"That's just a *Guinea pig*. For fifteen years I quit a health problem". Then I said to myself: 'No, I did. The first encounter with a girl you must never speak of your health, or this truncates right away every relationship!'

"Beautiful! Give me your data, so you contact. So I'll see if I can do anything" (I've never understood the significance of that "beautiful": it was addressed to my physical, or my illness?).

Afterwards, she studied; I fired using a laser, and helped me develop my powers. In fact, I helped develop others. In my opinion, not only is the prettiest, but it's also the best genetics in the world. Graduate with an "indefinable" vote, is already something. A number was supposed to receive, and that was, I think you have understood: 110 e lode!

Chapter II

Joann I have already submitted. Yes, my name is Mary Ivanovo. I prefer that you call me "the doctor".

As you may have read in the previous chapter, my friend and companion of adventure, Heart-Sun, is unique, even in her way of writing. Not allowed to write my biography, because I knew it would upset more than any of you readers. By the way, forgive him, if he were to have offended. He has done so, but is this we complete. Over time, we realized that something was there, and we made them inseparable. Me and him we complete each other.

As you are now already a scientist, geneticist. I am the daughter of Alex Kids (Алекс Бимби) and Anne Petite. Unfortunately, Mum Anne died in gives me birth. For my father it was not easy to get by psychologically, although he was a great scholar, hired by the Communist regime to develop more lethal weapons. With the death of her mother and my homeboy decided to flee abroad, and changed its name to Alexander Ivanovo (Иванов Александр), becoming a flounder to Anne's brother Ivanovo (Иванов Анна), and the famous pianist. His brother had disappeared, probably killed by any government agency. As an international spy, but he speculates that they sell to the Government the highest bidder. My father had him. He was arrested, and analyzes the best doctors. The answer? Says his medical record: "This man has lost irrevocably memory. Must have been through a lot, and don't recall ever her real past. We asked him to facts that only he could know, and don't remember a single one. Suffers from amnesia irrevocable, indefinite". I don't know how it was possible to save him at that time, but it is clear, now we are alive. I was a little girl, and I've never asked anything more to my father. Maybe someday, I can travel through time, and discover the truth ... but let's go back to talk to me.

I started to study DNA already when I was a child. I loved seeing those genetic strands that appeared on the books of my uncle, Dr. Peter Grant. He had married the sister of my father, Anne Ivanovo, a talented pianist. I still remember when my aunt teaching me a very difficult passage to the plane collided with the elbow my life. He noticed that I was becoming a woman and decided to tackle an issue that my father left my birth, I had not the courage to confront. So I asked her if I could deepen, borrowing the books of his uncle Peter. Still I didn't know that they were not really my uncles. To tell the truth, I discovered very recently. There mentioned Heart-Sun, but I don't think you will be noticed. I'll explain later.

I focused the study on pages dedicated to genetic changes during adolescence. In fact, there are many. The individual insemination is already written about DNA as will the physical changes; therefore, throughout life to change is not the DNA, but the physicist. Still, changes, in my opinion, could also be on the DNA. On the other hand I was only 9-10 years or so (Yes, I was very forward with the times in my physical; at school I was teased because I was the only "woman-child"). Today, I am sure that changes may occur on the DNA, and Heart-Sun I think is the most obvious example, along with another friend who soon knows.

Someone wondered if the three of us are super heroes, like those of comic books, because we are able to perform actions that no other human being seems to be capable of. In fact, all are super heroes, if they use their potential to the best of their abilities.

Who am I? I have only contributed to the construction of what is perhaps one of the most important inventions that this new century has had. On the other hand there are still ninety years of discoveries and inventions that bring top floor my invention. Do You See? I'm a super heroine? Tomorrow you'll read another book, and you have forgotten me. The fourth Chapter will be dedicated to this invention, which gave its title to the book.

In any case, Heart-Sun told you of that memorable day where we met, but did not explain everything. That morning I got a call from the University: I was informed that they would have arrived two men seeking genetic answers, and that I was the best student able to respond to their demands. In fact, not to brag, but those scholars prepare their genetics thesis at twenty-four years?

So I rushed to the bus (I know, grammatically it should write "automobile omnibus", but I prefer that everyone understand what I write). There, I met a strange boy, who brought a great change in my life. From that day on, we became inseparable. I still remember when I handed her the note with his phone number and email address: trembled so much, that I had the courage to tell him that I did not understand anything of what he wrote! I thought I wouldn't get offended if I ever more invoked. Moreover, it was the first time that we were seeing, and for me it could also be the last.

What a strange, during the bus ride, as we approached the last stop, I noticed that we were just us, in addition to the driver, of course. I did not believe my eyes, would also go to the same place where I had to go! Now I began to understand that the destiny we would definitely meet up, especially if he was a new student — off course definitely — of my school. He explained that I was studying there, and he replied: "That's great! This morning a strange phone call woke me up. An entry that I had difficulty understanding sound, why still asleep, she said: 'You are Mr. Rajok? ... Then you present at the University ... and, soon, because there's a job for you'. I didn't catch the name of the University, so I decided not to come, but then I found under the entry door of my house a sheet with the name of this school".

The description of the telephone resembled much to mine. Do you want to see that I should start a scientific research, and I had saddled him to an Assistant, a large ignorant, he wasn't even able to keep a job? I was tempted to come back home, but I knew that whatever would have happened that morning, it was essential to be in College, or I would have played at graduation.

I entered, and asked where I was waiting. Yes, he too was expected in the same room. There I met my professor of genetics, Genna'ro the Brand, and the author of the book that I had in my hands again, indeed, seeing him, the book I fell from the hands! Yes, was there present J. H. Klein! What an honor! As I saw him enter, and drop the book, asked me: "Miss, before you begin, there is something you would like to ask me? Behold, this is the first time I come to this city, and I visit the University. Do you think, on this occasion, I also brought my son? Thus, at the age of six, he entered the University. Maybe one day will choose this College to graduate". I had a thousand questions to extend, but Joann interrupted me: "Yes, I have one. Which means 'J. H.'?" What a stupid question! I wanted to ask a question, and he's going to throw on a question so trivial! He received no reply, and I couldn't ask my question, definitely smarter.

Professor The Brand explained to me that the University had accepted the proposal to take part in a Government project. Should be developed an object capable of reading the DNA of every living being. I still remember my response, which made a sensation in that room: "An object like that must be able to read the DNA of a nonliving, a stone, a Chair, and so on". Dr. Klein was appalled: "Miss, you — I'm sure — will make the entire project".

Joann interrupted us: "Excuse me, but I got into all of this? I don't understand anything about science. Then the incomprehensible genetics, DNA, but you're crazy? Is a university or hospital, this place? How do you say? One morning you get up out of bed, and take a decision, as I say, stupid. ... I hope your aim is not to make me become a Guinea pig!"

"No, none of that," said my professor. "We know that she is a computer enthusiast. Many students and professors have turned to her, on the contrary, many shopkeepers in the area we were made in his honor. Also on the Internet is considered as one of the most experienced in the world of computing. And I don't understand why not exploit this ability to find and keep a regular job!"

"In short, what should I do, write software to handle this strange project? I don't know any programming language. I only operate the majority of operating systems so perfect, even on a machine is not performing, and I also know to assemble and disassemble rubber-stamping a computer ... a moment because I have called? Should I run the software and help you put together this new contraption? If so, the New Technology attracts me and I like. ... And voilà! If I start, I know bring out even technical terms!"

We were all appalled! It was the smartest thing I had heard that morning, all the sentences you hear about from others and those spoken by me! Joann, perhaps, hidden real innate abilities!

My Professor and Dr. Klein said he couldn't explain better than that this work. You have already figured out what does, therefore, is the Rector's Office, where he can sign the contract.

And so it was that I had to put up with for the next months. Nevertheless at the end, I attacked, just as with a puppy dog or cat. Yes, dear, a caress and a small biscuit yet? I know, now I look like a mad scientist, but working with that guy could only mean madness. Yes, including that he would make me mad. And I'm madly I agreed to work together! To this day I do not know whether it was the best choice. I leave it to you to judge. Read the next chapters, and see you.

Soon enter our closest friend, who helped us find the answer too many questions.

Chapter III

Here I Am! No, I'm not the third protagonist of the story. I'm just a friend who helped our heroes to write their story. The problem now is that the third character is not easy to track down. Is constantly on the move. His travels did not allow you to get in touch at all times. So, we agreed that I talk about him. Then he will read these pages, and will decide whether they will or not lawful. Don't worry, what you are reading, has already been screened carefully by him, Tempest.

Talk about Tempest is the most difficult thing and intriguing, definitely. He is a man with unique capabilities. The DNA of his family has not undergone such change, that until now nobody is able to understand when he was born, nor at what time does he belong. In short, he is a man "timeless", yet he is able to bend time and space. It does, however, in a way that you wouldn't expect.

Three years ago, he still wasn't able to counterbalance its power. It was a morning of 2004 who managed to understand each other better. That morning had been brought by his father to a University. His father was a Professor of genetics with which to start a Government project. His father soon met the Professor, said: "This is the first time I enter this University. This morning my son has long insisted to accompany me. You know, this is the first time that I let my son come with me to these meetings".

At the head of this project, was placed the student Mary Ivanovo, assisted by a computer expert, Joann Rajok. During the interview, the child had to stay out of the room in which they were the four above, but for some reason, suddenly found him in with them. Inter alia, corporal was in a position a little detail: his hand was going to open a door, and leaving the room. To open the room, he saw a child, identical to it. He looked at his hands, and he noticed that had become suddenly large: he had become her father! An exchange of identity? A few moments later, continued to watch, but his gaze was not down to him as a child, but upward, towards himself and his father. What had happened? He was six years old and therefore smart enough you can begin getting questions. His father was a man under 30 years' old, married very young, and already a scholar, scientist of international fame. His father's name was J. H. Klein. The child's name was Vladimir.

The small Vladimir asked the father: "What happens?" The father replied: "Nothing, my son. We are well underway with this project. Be patient for a few minutes".

While Klein's father, professor The Brand and the younger Rajok were going into the Office of Rector to sign the contract, Vladimir came to the room, and asked

Dr. Mary Ivanovo: "You know what happens? Behold, it is the second time I go into this room".

"Are you sure? I know that I, your father, the Professor and Mr. Rajok we were the first to use this room, today. In addition, this is the first time you come here".

"I insist, I just now I was in here with all of you. I was my father".

The Doctor became speechless. The innocence of the child was the truth? The child was indeed was his father? No, the little fellow has six years, and has a lot of imagination. The doctor came to the little Vladimir, caressing his head, and was struck by a Flash of light. Looked around: he was in his bedroom, and it was morning, on his clock radio you were reading the 5.43. Near his bed saw little Vladimir who clutched a doll. Vladimir watched her, and said: "Hi, within a minute, you will receive a phone call. We will meet again later".

She squinted his eyes with his hands, and he saw the baby. Immediately after the phone rang. It was an invitation to start toward the University. There, he met the child again. In looking at it, he had a sense of *déjà-vu*. After the conversation in the room, the child re-enlisted, and said: "You know, today is the fourth time I enter this room. The first time I was my father, the second I came to bring you back home, the third I was again my father and now I am here for the fourth time ".

The Doctor realizes that that child lurked a non-standard DNA. Parse it, longed for but didn't want to talk about it with her father, to prevent uproar. On the other hand, the idea of analyzing a human being, as if it were a Guinea pig, did not belong to his vision of scientific research. Therefore decided to let stand.

Meanwhile, he saw the child begin playing with the doll that was carrying, was returning alone Dr. Klein. "This morning, I was in his bedroom. I woke up, and then we ended up here. We had the same conversation twice. Today I had to do a project for the study of DNA, and I discover that maybe there's something in me and my son who is wrong. Please, can you do something? I'll be your Guinea pig if you need! ".

The Doctor didn't know what to do at this point. He noticed that something odd was happening, and all in the same day. Had just known that funny guy. Now he had met this man and his son. The Doctor had no doubts: it was time to create a machine capable of reading DNA and his jokes. This machine also had to be able to find the genetic tree, similar to the tree, the individual selected for testing.

Chapter IV

After months of work, in which the Doctor couldn't focus soul and heart, since he also had the idea to prepare, were finally made progress. After about nine months of hard work, Mary graduated from Ivanovo, reaching the highest grades. The problem of new doctors or university graduates, usually, is tracking down a job. For you, this problem there was. He had already a researcher at the same University where he graduated. He could thus continue its work; the goal was to create a machine capable of decrypting the DNA. It was definitely easy. Finally, developed an object that resembled a gun.

On the barrel of the "gun", in place of the hole in order to escape the bullet, there was a special slide, from which he was fired a laser white. Usually where the bullets fall, there was a small door in which to place a digital memory. Pointing the gun toward any living being or to any object, the gun could scan his DNA. Then DNA was stored in memory. Under the gun was available a USB port for connecting a PC or a keyboard. Connect a keyboard; it was possible to write a name for the folder where you stored the genetic code shoots-flashed.

The gun received the name of "Genetic Scanner ™". The first Revision of the Scanner added a microphone, which allowed them to use special speech software to insert the folder name without requiring connecting a USB keyboard. We'll talk about later in the next Revision.

During the past year, Heart-Sun was really the Doctor's right-hand man. Throughout this time, he was a confidant: In addition to keep for himself all the information (which in any case would not have been able to repeat, being scientific and technical), had to take themselves all sentimental phrases that the Doctor said. In practice, after a few weeks, he seemed to have become a psychologist, to listen to their patients, rather than being a computer technician. Sometimes, he seemed to go mad, and then said: "Women are always women! Never having to do! ".

After his doctorate in genetics of Mary, he joined another team member, Dr. Klein, who, meanwhile, had managed to extricate himself more in his "power". Finally, he had managed to stay only in Klein adult, without moving in the body of my son. It was greatly aided by some letters that the Doctor's writing.

When the **Genetic Scanner** was finished, was tested on some items and on some laboratory guinea pigs, Klein asked if he could have read his DNA. The memory from 512 MB you burned it instantly. It was not enough to contain the genetic code of Klein. It was proven a 4 GB memory. This also burned, but only after finishing the scanning. Decided to try an 8 GB memory, even if the cost was very high. Not burned. The transfer to the PC Hard drive, however, was very slow; the PC also struggled a lot to read the text of the DNA. Klein, impatient, seemed to go on a rampage. There were two Thunders in a very short period. First Thunder seemed to disappear, but the second, reappearing. He had held at least a thousand sheets, bound. On these pages was written all over her DNA.

The other two were astonished: the PC was still processing data. It was possible; therefore, that he had them already? Explained that, when he had started to become frustrated, it was rediscovered in the future, at a time when PC's had just finished processing the data. Then printed them, this time without getting impatient. Once reprocessed data, managed to return the instant in which had disappeared.

The Doctor analyzed data: they were out of the normal. No other human being has a similar DNA data so rich! At one point, he noticed something: the DNA contained genetic data of a Klein from the future, but not by a few hours later, when the computer would have finished data processing, but future still more future, so future that would be unattainable within a normal life.

Klein said, "Doctor, you're right. During this time travel, I regained his memory. Now I understand why, when I came in this time, my memory is locked. By the way, from now on, call me Tempest ".

"Tempest?" asked Rajok. "'J. H. Klein'... and the 'T' where is he? Haven't you explained what do these initials, and now want to be called under a new name?"

"Boys, J. H. Klein that you know are just one of the many characters who throughout history have played. When I'm going for the next trip in time, you'll have to ask him that signifies his initials. This man you see now, I simply being hosted. The only thing I can tell you now is that every time I end up in the body of a member of the same family".

The Doctor said: "Interesting. It seems that you hide the DNA of an entire issue. Maybe you were born in an era where you can travel through time, and it has been implemented in your DNA this ability, perhaps with an improved version of our Genetic Scanner. Now we understand why you were blocked in our era, losing his memory".

Rajok said: "You stupid what you will say, but perhaps I have an explanation. Every memory that we inserted, it burned, right? Why? Because it was not sufficient to store the DNA data. It may be that the memory of the brain had been filled to the limit, and therefore it was deleted?".

"And how do you explain that both returned?"

"Simple, brain there must be some sort of *Trash* you save data before the final elimination".

"Joann, having spent a year with me, has turned into a scientist!"

Tempest interrupted them: "Unfortunately we never money for the in-depth study of the brain. We must stop the DNA. I will present me, if not I'll find a logical explanation".

Chapter V

Really I can return me to write? Or, how nice! Who knows why, but when I write I, there is always this word that is repeated.

Tempest said: "I saw you in the future, not only can, but must be scanned. I know you make great stuff, very soon, thanks to the power that you hide".

"Are you kidding? I hide a power? Watch that basket: it is full of handkerchiefs. There, every day we throw a dozen handkerchiefs, due to my chronic cold. The Doctor hasn't found time to look for a cure, but perhaps reading my DNA, finally ..."

"I know what your power is. I want you to find out. Doctor, scans him".

"Just a memory to 512 MB?" asked the Doctor.

"Yes, but with me there will an 8 GB".

After scanning, the memory was transferred into the computer. The development was rapid. The Doctor analyzed the results. Asked if we could be brought Tempest in a place open, but without people nearby, perhaps on the Grand Canyon. A few moments later, we were transferred to all three.

"How did you know you could carry us too?" I asked.

"A year ago, Tempest I transferred into space, leading me in my room ..."

"... And to what purpose? ... By the way, we moved only in space, or even over time?"

"Watching the clock!" I replied. Yes, the trip had occurred only in space. On Grand Canyon remained open-mouthed: he thundered! It was thus made clear why the name of Tempest. It was a pun. Each time he uses his powers in time and space, he thundered, sometimes causing a storm or a thunderstorm.

The Doctor explained why he wanted to go there. That was a perfect place to teach me how to use my powers. It was the ideal place also to receive my baptism of fire, i.e. my new name, Heart-Sun. Once finished, the Doctor asked me to blow on a handkerchief with the nose pointing towards the precipice.

In that, I saw him escape from my nose a strange liquid. I looked at my physical: he had become bigger. The clothes were tight. Yes, I was discovering a great deal of power hidden within me. I did not understand yet how I could use.

The Doctor asked him to take us forward in time, near a newsstand. I didn't understand the meaning. Arrived at newsstands, we noticed that it was passed a week. The

Doctor looked over the newspaper, because he wanted to find a criminal. He noted that on the day of our "departure" two people had entered the home of a granny, to steal money. The woman was in the House, and was murdered. The Doctor asked him to be transported to the previous moment in which the criminals were going into the House. We saw approaching two guys and a girl walk, while another was in the car. The Doctor wanted me to spray my liquid against the three guys and then against the door of the machine. In doing so, I saw three guys who stopped walking, and the other girl could not get out of the car: I had locked the door. Travel, froze the other ports. Yes, my liquid was powerful glue! We glued on the guys an inscription: "We wanted to Rob and kill the poor granny who lives in there, but we decided to stop us and be arrested." In that while, the Doctor asked me to spit from the mouth of spit, rather than shoot from the nose. The boys were no longer stuck! After that, we went back to the lab, and we controlled the newspaper a week later: there was more news!

There was however another report: that day, on the Grand Canyon, it was found the corpse of the Doctor! We had changed the future, but not in the way that we had hoped. Now we had to find out how to save the Doctor!

I suggested the doctor to take a new look at the DNA of Tempest. Printed data were changed, or rather; they were updated with the data of the trip! Yes, my intelligence was proving increasingly reliable.

Over the next few days, the Doctor spent some time studying fluids of my body, and I decided to hone my skills. Maybe, I was becoming a super-hero!

"My boy", I said "use Tempest, your powers wisely. We do not know who or what the death of Doctor Practice will. We must avoid it. Therefore, you do not fit your head, or you may become you the cause".

Chapter VI

The next morning, our friends did something special. Tempest had returned home because he had some family chores to be completed. Thus, in the lab, Heart-Sun asked the Doctor some explanations about his powers.

"Doctor, let's see if I've figured out how to work. Now therefore, I, being in direct contact of the Sun and, I think, of heat, become stronger, right?".

"Yeah, when you're in direct contact with the Sun, you absorb energy, which your body processes the way you've discovered yesterday."

"Well, here we are. Now, I ask you, we put the case that it is raining, or that it is a cool site ..."

"You couldn't use your powers ..."

"And in case of danger for two reasons I would risk to die: I'd be helpless, and then I the heart sick, and then I'd die of a broken heart".

'The sick heart?' you ask you who are reading. Eh, yes, our friend, Heart-Sun, has the heart sick. Unfortunately, his physique is pushed to continuous fainting, especially in times of stress. I know: in the first few pages, he forgot to tell you. In fact, I pointed out to him, but know that I responded? "We had decided that I was writing the first chapter, and so I did. What is written is written; do not change anything". I had to give in, partly because I was blushing, and you know what that means!

So, the Doctor suggested moving outdoors, since has been raining, to find out whether they could study the situation. When they exited, they meet strange people, who seized the Doctor, who was aiming for the Scanner to Heart-Sun, and then study the genetic changes on his physique in the rain. Now, Heart-Sun said: "Don't worry, everything is under control. It is not a real weapon. Is fake. We wanted to just take a test ".

Those men, however, were not students or university professors. They were intruders. They grabbed the Doctor, with the intent of a kidnapping! Heart-Sun didn't know what to do: in the rain, his powers were faded and, irony of name and time rainy, Tempest was absent!

"Doctor, I don't know what to do! I'm weakening! My heart is beating madly!". After I screamed, fought with his foot on the ground and the ground began to shake. The two men lost their grip, and the Doctor shouted: "Heart-Sun, save me! Only you have the strength to win! ".

Heart-Sun including having another hidden power. Immediately approached the men and, despite not having swelled unlike as is when it is under the Sun, was revealed to have a huge force. Tossed the two unfortunates on duty towards their car, inside which there was a third accomplice. The doors of the car were open, and the two entered. The car almost took flight, for the speed with which disappeared.

Heart-Sun was going to chase them, when he looked at the Doctor, lying on the ground. Came up. He was unconscious. Seemed to have been shot in the head. While the bore in the University's infirmary phoned, exploiting the speakerphone, Tempest, to warn of what had happened.

Tempest arrived literally in a heartbeat. When the Doctor awoke, the two friends would immediately know how he was. It felt good ... "Although that bump does not do justice to your beautiful face," said Heart-Sun.

After they were back in the lab, Heart-Sun had a question to ask: "How do you explain to me what happened?"

"There is much to discuss. Who knows who those men were? They were hooded, and so I do not know them in the midst of anybody ".

Tempest interjected: "I think it's important to find out who they were, because they might be the cause of your 'death', which we want to avoid. You said you wanted to steal your Doctor, right? ".

31

"Yes, I had grabbed it. They were really larger!"

"Maybe, their purpose is to steal you, forcing you to develop a weapon for them. Let's just hope they haven't managed to penetrate in the laboratory, during our absences, and therefore do not have stolen the formula Genetic Scanner ".

"There is a problem. Might not have been necessary to get in here, because data is also stored on your computer".

Feeling pulled in dance, Heart-Sun interjected: "Stop! Stop! I have super-protected PCs with which we work. All PCs are protected from hackers, crackers, bread and whatnot. Nobody can steal data electronically ".

"I hope you're right," says Tempest. "I don't know if you agree with me, but I would go back in time to find out if someone can be entered here without permission".

The Doctor interrupted him: "It wouldn't help anything. Remember that you can move just in time or in space, not in time and space. If not properly balance your moves, you could find yourself in the wrong place. We first analyze the video of surveillance".

Heart-Sun added: "The video surveillance, you said? Ahem! Maybe I don't know how they could keep an eye on. No one had spoken of their existence, and so was not protected!"

"Would you say that all this time we have been bugged, and we there we noticed? Then I come back in time, specifically the day you signed the documents, and we ask you to protect even videos. It will insert as clause in agreement".

The Doctor said, "No, don't do it. Our opponents might seek another way to how, maybe more violent".

"So, what do we do?" asked the two, astounding. "We cannot remain in its hands. We must react!"

"We can only try to discover who they are, and make sure there spying more, especially now that I was planning a new Revision of the Scanner".

"Another?"

"Yes, but I was working alone in my mind. I'm glad you haven't put anything in writing. ... Please, though, don't ask me anything about this new Revision, because I prefer the confidentiality, even on your part. Here at six days of my life will be endangered, and the fact that only I know certain information, could it be my salvation".

"You're right, and we will respect your decision. Nevertheless we can help you develop this new Revision?"

"Definitely, especially you, Heart-Sun, you will need to help with your technical abilities. I don't think I will serve others. ... Now, however, see to complete work on the cameras. When you're finished, in addition, we propose another thing".

After a couple of hours, Heart-Sun, helped by Tempest, finished the job. In this regard, do I have to tell you an anecdote? Whenever Heart-Sun was wrong to touch the wires, and therefore took a Jolt, forced Tempest to go back in time. Tempest every time he repeated: "It is not a video game, in which restart from last saved!" In the meantime he enjoyed, because time travel, Heart-Sun was the tremendous roar of Thunder. Who knows if it was better to shock or the ROAR?

When they finished the work, the Doctor suggested to whittle and dub footage taken from those of the previous months, and ensure that their "love" indicator lights will undergo information "stolen", but inaccurate. They were all in agreement. While the Doctor and Heart-Sun began assembling the video, Tempest went forward in time, to when the two friends ended up working a couple of days later and recovered a copy of the video. He went back in time, and inserted these files to a PC, which charged the computer hackers.

During the work, instead of Tempest, was J. H. Klein and Heart-Sun had attempted to ask that question that kept itself by a year, but there was another even more important: "What happened to me this morning in the rain while we were struggling for survival?"

The Doctor explained to him that the Sun and the rain gave him two types of different powers. Under the Sun, heat, become larger and, at the same time, the body will digest the waste, ready to use via the mouth and nose. The waste attached to the nasal septum, liquids, absorb the fluid have been transforming into a paste. The fluid was called "liquid pasting". From the mouth instead escapes a liquid that can dissolve the glue, a "BREW mug". The enlarged body also comes from the growth of muscles, thus increasing physical strength.

And capabilities in the rain? The Doctor did not provide me the correct explanation, in fact, it was I, when we met, to help you find the answer. She simply said that the fall of temperature not allowed him to become bigger or to dissolve the body fluids. Perhaps, though, the rain, being a fluid, became a middle ground between "pasting" and "liquid infused jug". That explanation is wrong! You want to know? Read on, and discover the day we met.

It took two days to explain a Heart-Sun all these things, because, as you know, "I don't understand anything about science, especially genetics." In fact, the two days of explanations were mainly due to the fact that they were doubling the footage, and therefore had little time for conversation. Dr. Klein, for two days, they had a lot to see the Doctor rack your brains to explain in the simplest way to Heart-Sun these things.

There is now a fact to explain, what you read, is then changed by the return of Tempest. Fortunately, somehow, we managed to recover this historic moment as amended by time travel. Upon his return, Tempest brought back the finished video, which was posted in the outgoing server. Afterwards, Tempest decided to take two days of freedom, and so traveled over time, for two days, leaving the other two comrades in adventure at the mercy of Dr. Klein and a new future that surely was not very different from what you have read above.

Chapter VII

Over the two days, finally Tempest returned, and all three were working on the new project. There were still four days. Unfortunately, Tempest in those two days had to live in a different era, otherwise his alter ego, Dr. Klein, could not remain in the lab to dub himself in videos. Who knows that time visited? I want to ask?

Also Heart-Sun had in mind this question, and notice what happened when he opened his mouth, therefore: "Dear friend, then as you walk? You're back, eh? I wonder where you have been all this time. Would you tell us? Would you tell us that you combined? If you find any nice girl to be saved? ...".

"I have entered into the life of Vladimir!"

"By whom?"

"Really, after working for months together, you don't know who Vladimir is?"

"No, why should I know?"

Shortly it took because the two came to blows. I don't know who would win. Stop! Better change speech!

The Doctor interrupted them, saying: "So, we want to get down to work? We have only four days to build the **Revision 3.0** Genetic Scanner, and before they kill me!

Have you taken a look at the newspaper? The news hasn't changed at all! Is always the same, and I don't even like the idea of being photographed on the front page, dead ".

"Sorry, dear, stop immediately, and get to work. From where do we start? ".

"We have to build another pistol identical to **Revision 2.0.** Then we will add a new and powerful tool ".

"Do you want to become a real gun?"

"I have asked the confidential. ... Thank you, Tempest, for going back in time, not forward, to find out what this invention, though perhaps you already know what it is".

"Hey! It is not right, he can travel through time, and I am the only ignoramus here inside!"

The Doctor said, "Shut up, rather you should thank him for having stopped in our time, to help us".

Tempest said: "I feel compelled to tell you one thing. What we do in the next four days, and the salvation of Mary, are essential for the salvation of the whole human race".

"What?" exclaimed Heart-Sun?

"In future, we will talk a lot these days. Before finding myself stuck in your time, I visited a future era in which it was explained clearly that these days on the Grand Canyon would be a tremendous thing happened that would change forever mankind".

"My death?"

"No, because the books of science spoke about you for a long time after. When the other day we did go to the Grand Canyon, I thought that was the day X, instead it seems to be success anything".

"Tell me, could we get this Revision? I can think of no other invention. Could this change to Genetic Scanner be the cause? Maybe you were back in our time to help build it? So, not succeeding, I kill you?"

"I don't know ... do you think the changes that we're keeping hidden, dangerous?"

Heart-Sun broke off dialogue: "Tempest, you'll keep an eye out over the coming days. Never leave thee ever hurt her ".

Tempest answered him: "You could be its threat, with your powers".

Once again, the Doctor said: "Enough! Lately been always fighting. You seem jealous of each other's powers. I think each of you two has developed the powers so that they may be used to do well, not to quarrel. And, if you have different powers and you are in the same team, to me, means that jointly should be used".

Tempest asked: "Are you saying that we would be just a bad twist of fate? Do you remember that I can change the times and, perhaps, the seasons, traveling through space and time".

"No, I'm not talking about the destiny already written. I'm sure everyone build their own destiny. What I meant is, in short ... I meant that each of us exists in this world in their position. I am a scientist, who is helping to develop and manage your powers. You are different people from the rest of human beings. Maybe you hope to mankind at this time"

Heart-Sun broke into an exclamation worrying, with the newspaper of the future in his hands: "Hey! Look here! Tomorrow night will be a huge disaster! We must prevent these two trains ticket! Perhaps, if we can change the future of the two trains, we change the Grand Canyon!"

"Joann" replied the Doctor. "When you put, seems really a leader!"

Heart-Sun replied theatrically: "Thank you! Thank you!", smiling.

Our three friends had a few hours to complete the new invention and to avert disaster, and also needed rest! While Heart-Sun and the Doctor worked to Revision 3.0,

Tempest has projected the following day, but ended up in the body of W. A. Klein, the father of J. H., Vladimir's grandfather and great musician. It was in the body of an eighth-year-old, slow to hear and to move. Grandfather Klein, fortunately, was traveling in a convoy, one of two trains that had collided! Good luck or bad luck for Tempest? He noticed that in the midst of the Rails there were strange crevices, and not far from there, he saw his son J. H. with Heart-Sun and the Doctor who tried to save the train: it was raining, and Heart-Sun therefore had the power of rain. He was jumping to invite the locomotive engineer to stop the train. However, in doing so, he was breaking Rails. Here is the cause of the accident. Tempest had to hurry up and go back to warn Heart-Sun that he would have been the cause.

When was transported back in time, he noticed a particular second train wasn't there! What he had done? Was going to happen a disaster, in which only one of the trains involved was found. Decided not to go back in time, but moving through space, to find out what was happening. Came with his three friends.

"Dad, what are you doing here?"

"I'm not your father but Tempest".

"Now let me explain why you were entered into me. But why don't you choose me?"

"I think that the goal was not to save the trains, but your father. Maybe your father has the answers you're looking for to know what will happen the day after tomorrow. Anyway, where is the train? ".

"We managed to get it to stop further".

"Very well, unfortunately, this train is bound to go off-roading. Heart-Sun, I will try with my powers to bring forward a few hours in order to find out whether the storm that I will spring manages to take away the rain and let you buy your muscles to stop the train. Start racing meeting. See you later".

Yes, Tempest managed to sweep away the clouds and sunshine. Heart-Sun managed to stop the train and save dozens of lives.

When Tempest returned to another time, could explain how to save the two trains. In the hours after he completed the Revision 3.0. Unfortunately I still don't know the answer more awful: how to save Mary, the Doctor? Maybe could help them though grandfather Klein. As a result of a phone call, they decided to meet at the site of another meeting.

After saving the train, ousted Grandfather Klein. Heart-Sun promptly lost no time, and asked: "Excuse me; I know that she is called W. A. Klein? What do these initials?".

"Heart", as you're rude ", exclaimed the Doctor.

"Don't worry Miss," said Grandfather Klein. "My name is Wolfgang Amadeus Klein and I was born the same day of Mozart. My father would call me like that musical genius".

"His son is named after a famous musician? J. H. Klein ... What do they mean?"

"Boy, my son is here, why don't you ask him?"

"He doesn't know how to respond. Does not know".

"Like, boy? I am Dr. J. H. Klein ..."

"Played by Tempest".

"Tempest? Truly, he is not here. "

Grandfather Klein intervened: "My boy, you hide a fire inside of you! You have to become more patient, if you want to reach my age".

"Behold, the future we would like to talk to her," Mary intervened. "I am Dr. Mary Ivanovo. Someone wants to kill me, and I don't know tell me why. Within two days, I might find myself on the Grand Canyon, corpse!"

"Miss, we are very far from that place. Today is the first time that the sky clears up these parts, after a month of continuous rains"

"And yet, a few days ago they tried to rob me, and I'm sure they want to kill me!"

"Tell me miss, what is his job? Is Dr. at some hospital?"

"No, I'm a researcher at a University. I'm making an important genetic research".

"I understand. When I was a kid, my father told me that one day would arrive this time. He told me that I had to thank for having saved. And, in fact, all these people that she's with her friends she saved should thank you very much. If I recall correctly, my father told me that today I would have shot her. I never realized that would mean this. If you saved me, I don't think I will shoot."

"Maybe I didn't understand. She'll be the first person with whom I will experiment my new invention. You will feel heat from a laser. This laser will read his DNA. Let's see who tells me the notebook. She has a normal DNA! Dr. Klein, let me try with his DNA. His DNA indicates that she is Tempest! Answer me: is or no Tempest?"

"No, I'm J. H. Klein".

"This means that became Tempest today! Today she has acquired the powers! This is a memorable day! Why was stuck at this time, was not yet Tempest. Now we will insert in the Scanner data from Tempest via USB. Mr. Klein, now tester for the first time the new feature".

"That happens to me? Help, I feel weird? Ah!". Broke a thunder, and Grandfather Klein fell to the ground, unconscious. "Doctor, you killed my father!"

"No, he is not dead, feel its pulse on the wrist," replied Mary. "I think this was the first time that Tempest has traveled through time". After a moment, Grandfather Klein is straightened.

"Miss, she is in grave danger! In his lab, there is a man who wants you to accomplish things horrible, which will then be killed!"

"Who is it? Knows what it's called?"

"I do not know. I just know that I found myself in the future! And before he could get back into this, I had a strange dream. I met a man, a Spanish merchant. Was in a port. From its cargo, a rhinoceros was chasing me, and he shouted: 'Take it to the Horn! '. This made me remember why my son has changed his surname, and continues to say that my name is W. A. Klein. Instead I'm Wolfgang Amadeus Klein Horn! My son called Johann Klein Horn".

"Well, but this will allow me to save me?"

"Miss, check the newspaper which has with itself".

"Yeah, it's gone the article train crash. Instead, it reads that the legendary Dr. Livings will give a lecture at my

University! That honor. We see that says this article: 'A Conference on genetics and Africa was marred by the discovery in the afternoon the body of Dr. Ivanovo. It is not yet clear how her body could reach the Grand Canyon in so few hours. Someone suggested that the Conference was an impersonator. Of course the article on my death remained unchanged".

Dr. Klein commented: "Livings? A Conference? You don't know anything. Maybe the thing was kept hidden because Dr. Livings feels threatened? Maybe, try to save him she might be killed".

"No, we cannot allow that to happen. We must return to the laboratory immediately!"

Chapter VIII

Before continuing the story, it is right that we speak of Dr. Livings. This man is one of the greatest researchers of African people. We get step by step. It seems that before ten years ago, no one knew of its existence. The most accepted legend is as follows.

About ten years ago, the Italian Government entrusted to a group of Venetians as investigators discover what was happening in an Amusement Park.

Should be based on a report which said simply: "The African Carousel under construction is producing many deaths. The African Safari may close. Problems encountered in the largest Amusement Park of Continent, located by the Lake ".

Using a little logic, suggested that the problem was located at Gardaland, Amusement Parks most beloved by the Italians. Moreover, their, Venetians, were close to the Park and Lake Garda. Inside the Park, in fact, there was an attraction called the "African Safari". There was a problem: this attraction has existed for more than ten years, and it does not appear that he ever caused fatalities.

They asked the Italian Government explanation. The carousel was under construction in Africa, more specifically in Tanzania! Never would come from those phrases damaged or broken.

So, they left for Tanzania, for a trip fraught with dangers and revelations. Specifically, it started at the vast Lake Tanganyika. At Rukwa Region, was under construction an amusement park, Tanganikaland (?)

Unfortunately, since the beginning of the work were made many accidental deaths, perhaps too many to be considered such. They started investigations. It was clear: too much closeness with the Democratic Republic of the Congo was the cause of the deaths. They suggested block jobs, and to transfer the Park further north, perhaps to Kigoma, which lies on Lake. The proposal was not accepted, because the project involved a reconciliation of the populations. In addition, for months, went ahead with negotiations for the release of a man, mulatto.

The three investigators therefore decided to do their part. They began negotiations for the release. This could only happen on condition that the park is maintained for 50% by the Government of Congo. According to them, the thing was OK, if this would eliminate bloody disputes. The thing was accepted.

The man was released. What was his name? Dr. David Livingstone! No, this is the same David Livingstone lived in the 19th century. It was however a descendant. There is a legend about this: the first Doctor Livingstone would leave a child in Africa, at the Tanganyika Lake, because they form a lineage of Scots. From this seed, David Livingstone II would arrive.

David had never exited from Africa, but had turned the whole continent. He graduated in Political Science, Psychology and Education Sciences in Cape Town. After graduation, he presented a project to bring peace and unity in Africa: the construction of parks for families. The first of these was to be Tanganikaland.

When work began, was kidnapped by some Congolese rebels, who wanted to conquer that slice of Tanzania. Inter alia, this nation bordering the Congo, but also with Rwanda and Burundi, the scene of bloodshed.

The fate of Dr. Livingstone seemed marked. After his release, he completed the work, although he had to hire three Venetians as bodyguards. Finally, he chose to change his surname to Livings. It is said that he is one of the greatest storytellers, connoisseur of the finest and most recondite African legends. The knowledge of this man would fill whole libraries.

Chapter IX

Our friends back in the lab, the next day, we found the professor The Brand that was holding in his hand a new camera. He explained that he wanted to prepare a few photographs of the most well-coordinated scientific team who knew. The photographs were to be hung in strategic places, given the imminent arrival of Dr Livings.

The Professor made a photo of each of their three, namely Dr. Mary Ivanovo, Dr. J. H. Klein (or Johann Klein Horn) and the young technician Joann Rajok. After the professor The Brand went off, the three said: "It seems that the room temperature is suddenly increased and decreased". There were however no weight.

Was the last day to provide an escape route for Dr. Livings, in case of an attack, but also an escape for Mary! Mary asked Tempest: "Please, if I die, don't take me on the Grand Canyon. So we'll be sure that article in the newspaper will change, although not in the way we wanted".

"I will do everything to avoid your death. In the event, I will return back in time".

"No, don't do it. If it were to happen, I have changed the future of which I have talked about the other day!"

"Guys!" interjected Heart-Sun, "I had an idea for tomorrow. I would like to fit around the podium a shatterproof glass. You, my darling, you will be protected, but also Dr. Livings will be protected".

Had a few hours to do it, and also do not want anyone else to know. So, they rode the glass on the sly during the next night.

Made preparations for security, there remained a speech still open. Now all three knew what served the Revision 3.0, at least theoretically.

Heart-Sun asked the Doctor: "I seemed to understand that you have given birth to Tempest and that his real name is Wolfgang Amadeus Klein Horn, right?"

"I don't know. Looks like it's gone as well, but he was the one to ask. Now I am very confused".

"I have another question: at least for a period of his life, Tempest was normal — had no powers. Then, before I meet you I had no powers! As I explain this thing? It is not that you have flashed me too?"

"What? ... No, you cannot. We built together with the Revision 3.0, in the last week. You know very well. And then, I have given birth to power in Tempest, but there are two issues that should be explained. The first: I had already provided his DNA altered. He just put it at the disposal. I simply inserted into its DNA! In short, I returned it to him".

"I'm not seeing much, but you're the scientist, and you certainly are right. Tell me what the other issue is".

"The other concerns his ability to cause storms and tempests. He was already able to before you know. You've not noticed? Did it rain for a whole month, and then stopped suddenly rain!"

"Would you say that every 'Klein non-Tempest' that we met, she was already able to intervene on time?"

"Yes, thanks to the laser, all quiet now is able to handle the weather and that related to the flow of events".

"In essence, the new Genetic Scanner you can put evens his powers in me or him mine?"

Tempest the interrupted, saying: "I do not agree. Okay do not give either side lacks genetic powers, but now we can contribute to the cure of various diseases. Rewriting the DNA of a sick person, you can cure your disease!"

"Yes, this is a lawful, but the problem is that we're still on an experimental basis. It will take some time, before being sure that we will be able to heal all diseases. But now I realize how this week may have changed the future of mankind. Thanks to the three of us, we found an almost definitive care!"

Tempest retorted: "I don't see why you should die at this point. I don't owe anything to stop, because you haven't built a weapon but a wonderful machine. I think that tomorrow, after saving you and professor Livings, I can resume my trips to explore time and space. My job is almost done".

"I'm so excited, that would put me into tears" theatrically, Heart-Sun. "I would propose one thing: why not talk about it tomorrow with professor Livings? Reportedly he's the best connoisseur of African cultures, and surely of disease".

Tempest replied: "Yes, I believe that my time here is about to take place. You are become more mature, and you, Doctor, you'll have a partner that will support much longer. In the future your names will always be placed close together".

The Doctor replied: "Would you say that we intended to get married? I'll change the future, don't worry".

Chapter X

"Sorry if I interrupt you, but can I tell you?" A mustachioed, blond, dressed in suit and tie, entered the lab. "They asked me to be here to participate in an important scientific experiment. I was running around the campus. Tell me that I have come to the right place, finally!".

Tempest positively affronted replied: "It depends on what he is looking for."

"I know that this is an experiment to test various securities, in short. I know I will receive a small allowance and a certificate".

Heart-Sun turned silently to the Doctor: "Why not shoot-flash?"

"No, we don't have to use so the Scanner!"

"Come on, let's enjoy some"!

Tempest asked this young man: "What's it called?"

"My name is John Little Horn".

"You are Romanian?"

'No!'

"You are Russian?"

"No! Ah! Ah! I'm English!"

"You are English?"

"Yes. My last name means 'small horn'".

"'Little Horn'?" interjected Heart-Sun, "did you say?"

"Yes, it means 'small horn'".

"What a coincidence! My name is Joann Rajok, and even my last name, translated from Russian, means 'small horn', and my English name is John!"

Tempest intervened: "We are too! My name is Johann Klein Horn, i.e. 'John Small Horn'. That curious we are three people in here with the same name, albeit from three different countries!"

The Doctor said, "Might not be a coincidence. Perhaps each of you has a role in this story! In any event, Mr. Little Horn now isn't planning any experiment. We invite you however to show up tomorrow morning to the Conference with Dr. Livings".

"The legendary Dr. Livings will be here tomorrow? I don't want to miss this Conference. I will certainly".

Didn't understand why Dr. Klein and Joann would accompany me right out. Only then I understood they had to keep myself away from their plans for the next day's safety. They couldn't trust me. Could be I the terrorist!

While I was out, I saw two hooded men approached. Hit me, making me roll the stairs outside the entrance of the University. When I got up, I saw them start to fight with two new friends. Immediately began to rain, and Joann fought ashore, which immediately made me tremble. He grabbed for hands the two "gentlemen", which he did fly away. Then I went next door, and I was naturally telling him: "You have a great strength, but you have to be careful not to try too hard, the beating of your heart has become very strong!" Looked at me with his eyes, weird and then burst out laughing. Professor Klein asked me to return, and brought me back into the laboratory.

Dr. Ivanovo did not believe his eyes: I was back! The three I came with their names by battle: the Doctor, Heart-Sun and Tempest. I explained the story of the powers of the two men. I asked if the Doctor, having chosen a name for the battle, had some power. She replied no. Then, I proposed to get myself a battle name, JLH, which are my initials. I bought all of them. They wanted to know if I was in cahoots with those two, if I was working as a terrorist on my own, or I was the unlucky guy. In particular, Heart-Sun asked me:

"You have a super hearing. You hear the beats of my heart!".

"Well, I think we would hear anyone, are very strong when you get close to another person. In any case, as a good musician, I know have a superfine ear".

"That's why your name was familiar to me," said Tempest. "Klein Wolfi has directed your music?"

"Yes. Wolfi would your father, right?".

"Yes, it is so affectionately called by Mom Leopoldina".

"Guys, it's not a super hearing. These are the words of an expert geneticist who I am".

"Quite, why not shoot-flash to give us reason?"

"No need, I'm sure."

"You haven't already flashed?"

"Yes and no".

"Like Yes and No?"

"I must admit one thing. As you know I consider one of the most experienced scientists in the field of genetics. And there's a good reason. I have a power that ye know not: I cannot read a person's DNA. I don't know how this happens, but whenever anyone approaches me, I can't figure out if its genetic tree hides the DNA modifications, hidden powers. I could just write a new DNA, nothing more".

"From the left a little Flash, so you'll be at the Club".

"Joann! Who are these ways? We must not use our capabilities as pride, but for the benefit of others", said Tempest.

"Don't worry; I will remain as they are. Rather, just now I have explained the operation of your powers. I'm not entirely in agreement on how to develop the power of Heart-Sun. I'm a musician, and I believe he understood what will become strong in the rain. Probably, your heart begins to beat following the rhythm of the rain. This rate allows you to decide how much force to that point. If near you there is Tempest, he may increase or decrease your strength. Therefore, you see of getting along, you two!"

"Finally someone supports me in my campaign to do good these two! You know, JLH, I think you have really no reason. You are not gifted, but are equipped with a unique sensibility. I think you can get into the team. Tomorrow you will be able to give us a hand, in the likely battle that breaks out in here ..." At this point, I reported the facts of the last days, and what should have happened the next day.

Chapter XI

The next morning, at 7.00 o'clock, two cars broke through at the same time as the gates of the University. One was led by Heart-Sun and the other to the Doctor.

As soon as you saw, the Doctor exclaimed, incredulous: "You seem the way to arrive at a Convention? You are in Jeans!"

"Look, I've spent a lot of time to decide how to dress! Knowing that maybe there will be getting dirty, this today, thought I'd equip myself! And then, with my powers, why should I mess up a smart dress?"

At that time, "appeared" Tempest, who quickly realized that air would pull. Heart-Sun rebuked for his choice, but he remembered that day had something else to worry about! While the Doctor and Tempest thickening towards the University entrance, Heart-Sun called the two, saying: "Look here!" And he opened the door of his car. Lying on the back seat, there was a complete.

"Now, let me time to change," he said. For once, he was right! For once, he could not let him fool! Meanwhile they closed the door, pulled a strong wind, which made the door hard to close. He was spontaneously using both hands, and so the dress fell to the floor. What a disappointment! Was dirty! If he had worn the dress at home, would not have to open and then close the door: so, would not have dirtied his precious!

Pity that I arrived only to 8.00! I missed the show. In any case, Heart-Sun begged Tempest to go back in time, to fix it. Tempest refused, but the Doctor suggested he returned back, Yes, but at home of Heart-Sun. Tempest said, "you know full well that if I move over time, I can't even go into space, and therefore to decide where to go. The only thing I can do, is prevent fall dress ... by the way, there is a nice puddle near the entrance of the University: in my opinion, Heart-Sun we would drop the suit the same ..."

"Tell me, Tempest, have traveled through time to discover all the ways I'd soiled her dress, to choose then the most humiliating?"

Finally, Tempest went back in time. From where he stood, moved into the home of Heart-Sun, and so explained that would happen. Heart-Sun did not accept the suggestion to leave already dressed as a House, and therefore decided to get the same in Jeans. This time he managed to avoid the crash, but the clothes fell in puddle. Tempest was amused: he was right! He agreed to go back a moment, and Heart-Sun helped bring the clothes inside. Thank goodness that Tempest has a very good memory, and thus can tell us all what he sees in his temporal shifts. The only thing we don't know is whether exaggerates. We should find someone else or someone else capable of time travel. Yes, but whom? Do you think that there is anyone else? Either there is enough!

So, I arrived at 8.00. Entering the lab, I attended a very interesting dialogue between Heart-Sun and the Doctor.

"Doctor, from the day I met you, I must bring a question".

"I'm trying to guess which deep thought will be contained in your question. Please, give me your question".

"Why do you like so much green? You dress always green. Need to take chunks out of hope, or remind you that you are poor? ". In fact, on that day, the Doctor was just dressed in Green: Green shoes, green socks, green skirt, green shirt, green suit, green enamel, green lips, green earrings, and green clip.

"Thanks to this job, I'm not at all. Consequently, it is the other choice: Yes, I'm really hopeful to do studies that will improve the lives of mankind. And your contribution so far has been really valuable. Satisfied?".

"Yes." ... Oh! Looks a bit, it's our friend JLH".

"Good morning to all", I said.

"You too, though, joke: a really great outfit", said all three in chorus.

"Thank you, thank you ... and you, dear Tempest, how come you chose to dress ... 19th century?"

"Yeah, you're really *in*, fashionable, with prehistoric that dress," added ironically the usual Heart-Sun.

Tempest said, "Dear Heart-Sun, you should know that for once I wanted to do what jokes with others. I was in the old 19th-century London to know Herbert George Wells. You all know who he is, right? I explained to him that, unlike written by him, I don't need a time machine to travel. I myself am a time machine. I took a walk through time, in particular in the future. So he found the inspiration for his famous novel. To ensure you haven't altered the story, I compared the book in the library of the University with the Edition on display since before our meeting in London. You haven't changed one iota. So, Yes, I was inspired to compile the book. In return, they offered me the complete that I'm wearing now, provided, however, that it is returned at the end of the Conference".

I asked him: "Sorry, why didn't you bring with you? So we would have known".

Tempest replied with a serious tone: "I did, and it was killed even before the Conference began. I went back in time, and I decided that H. G. Wells must not participate in this convention".

Our dialogue was interrupted for a few minutes, with the arrival of two men, who were presented to me. To tell the truth, one of the two was presented to all four of us. He was the professor The Brand, type, with a smile and a bit of beard on his face, and doctor Livings.

Professor The Brand also wore a suit similar to mine. Who knows why, but I expected a man dressed in a toga and a square hat on his head. Even for idea. He was really cute. The Professor made me just some jokes: "Hey, mustache! She wants me to compete. Do you see on the floor, in the minutes leading up to the start of the Conference? I brought one with him, right? Her dress has many pockets ... "and other similar phrases.

Dr. Livings also had an exaggerated stereotype: I see get a type to Indiana Jones, who wore a shirt with no tie, pants with tips from elephant, and maybe even a rope around the shoulders. Instead, he was dressed in white, with a bow tie instead of the tie. Had its English air, in memory of his ancestor (although, to tell the truth, was Scottish).

At the beginning of the Conference was missing about half an hour. Dr. Livings, a man renowned for his extensive knowledge of African legends, approached Dr. Ivanovo, to tell a story. Took her aside and told her: "Nearly five hundred years ago a man had become famous in Nairobi, Kenya. It was considered a demi-God, why has hunting an animal very difficult to capture and even more to kill: the rhino. It is said that he used to rip these animals, horns before inflict the final blow. One of these horns was then bought by a European. From this was born a flower Horn. This flower became the symbol of his family. It is said that whoever ..."

The story was interrupted abruptly by a blow on the shoulder by the professor The Brand: it was time to start toward the Auditorium.

Chapter XII

The day before, the Auditorium was equipped with defense to ensure safety at the oblivious doctor Livings and Dr. Ivanovo. The Rector of the University came to the podium to introduce the Convention.

"Good morning to all of you who have been invited to this very important meeting? Today will be a very important summit, where Dr. Livings we will present the results of his research lasting for at least ten years. The theme of the speech he will deliver to us is: 'Anthropology and DNA in Africa'. Before you leave the word, though, The Brand, Professor of our University there somewhere delivers a keynote".

"Introducing Dr. Livings for me is truly a great honor. This man has studied the secrets of life; he toured Africa during his lifetime, researching in the field. It's definitely the expert of all stories and legends related to the African world. Also has the knowledge of several African languages. Before leaving the word it is essential to explain why he came here, at our humble College. However, I am pleased to announce that for about a year, the University has accepted the proposal of a governmental project under the supervision of Mr. Klein. This project was executed so dear by Dr. Ivanovo. At the moment, we are not yet able to provide you with the details, but I can tell you that have conducted important studies relating to DNA decoding. Maybe, thanks to these studies, all the secrets of human DNA, inanimate, vegetable and animal can be unraveled. Nevertheless we'll get step by step. The time has come that I can be silent, and let the word to her, Dr. Livings".

"Dear, you want me tell you? Before you speak of scientific topics, difficult, many of you should struggle to comprehend, let me tell a joke. I was the year 1099. A man, Hassan-i Sabba'h, was the chieftain of a tribe Ishmaelite, who resided between Damascus and Antioch, precisely to Alamu't, the mountains of West-Central Iran. That was the era of the Crusades. He was told the Old Man of the Mountain. All members of the tribe were forced to utter obedience. To hit its ideological and political enemies, Hassan-i Sabba'h used a weapon that was not used against them, but they did use. This weapon was called *Hashīshiyyūn* (نيشاشـحـ, 'addicted to hashish'). The Crusaders, unable to correctly pronounce this word, called the members of this tribe 'assa'ci', especially after he succeeded in capturing Jerusalem. Today, we all know that hashish, or cannabis, is a psychoactive drug. The Italians seem to have been the first to turn this word 'murderer' (*'assassi'no'* in Italian; literally *'assassin'* in English).

"You'll wonder why introduce myself with a similar story. However, the words over the centuries have changed meaning, and often a sense of original use. The first to use those words today no longer exist, but their descendants are here, in our midst. Usually, people are unaware of their descendants, still in their DNA hide an encyclopedia it would be wonderful to decipher and study. Until today, man has used the family tree to know the origin of his family. My studies were aimed to know the genetic tree of mankind. You see everyone hides in itself similar but unique genetic data at the same time. Each Member of the same family has similar DNA, with some variables that make each unique family. Each new generation enhanced DNA with never-before-seen data: those ancestors and those of the new born. Each child thus enriches the DNA of parents and predecessors of the same family. Borne in mind that, you can assume that anyone who seems to become murderer naturally have written into their DNA that at least his ancestor had become an assassin by necessity, consequently changing the fate of his offspring. Maybe it was a woman, who begat a son in jail, and this was brought to an orphanage and adopted by a family, changing forever the House. This means that the study of the genetic tree might prove more reliable than pedigree.

"Imagine a descendant of Hassan-i Sabba'h today, who does not know to be from that tree, perhaps because that genetic pedigree has been discontinued. Maybe it has murderous tendencies, and does not know how to explain the reason. Maybe he has a craving for the drug, and doesn't understand why.

"These are all theories that the research of Dr. Ivanovo may confirm, modify or deny. From the first data collected, however, I can attest that a lot has already been confirmed. In any case, before knowing our origins, such as most important and noble use could be made of these findings? Certainly, knowing the genetic tree if our ancestors suffered from some illness, and therefore prevent and cure; maybe even change your DNA, so reset all information concerning the negative aspects of his past. Yes, DNA hides a world that could be called ' parallel '.

"Unfortunately the human history shows that with the enrichment of data in the physical human DNA has undergone significant changes, negative. This is not instead occurred in animals, of which the DNA has not changed over time. This inter alia proves with certainty that evolution cannot be completed. Let me explain to you, however some details.

"When God created man, human DNA was perfect. After the original sin, man began his journey to achieve catastrophic results. The first men could live almost a thousand years. But it seems that nobody has managed to overcome Methuselah ("Man of the Missile") who lived 969 years. The same Adam, we know that lived 930 years. I just read the fifth chapter of Genesis to find this data. To live so long surely men were healthier.

"So let's move on to the next step. Soon, they began to register the first cases of disease in men. It seems that, thanks to the Mosaic Law, Jews were potentially healthier people of antiquity. I say potentially because, in reality, often disobeyed the Law. In the Law, in several places we read how to treat cases of healing from one of the most famous ancient diseases, leprosy. It should be noted that the law was written about 1,500 years before the coming of Christ on Earth.

"We are now at the time of Jesus Christ. We read in the Gospels that, frequently, lepers were Jesus to be healed miraculously. Once, they even ten. It seems that DNA had undergone another modification: leprosy, humans could no longer heal without a miracle or the use of drugs such as those used today.

"All this shows clearly that more time has passed, and more human DNA began to contain harmful information. I thought that the millennia have inserted DNA too much data, and so this caused the slowdowns at the sympathetic system with regard to decrypt all data quickly. ... By the way, now it is better that we make a break. I put too many irons in the fire. I recognize that you need to consider".

Chapter XIII

The audience was speechless. No one seemed to have noticed that the Rector had disappeared. When Dr. Livings went up on the podium, the Chair of Rector was a hooded man. Because the Chair was beside Dr. Ivanovo, we three, we assumed that he had identified the terrorist. We were confident that if they had noticed her too. But we had to decide quickly. Indeed, they had to decide how to act. I was there inert.

Tempest moved quickly through space, and approached the man hooded. Meanwhile, I noticed that the entire audience had suddenly asleep. At the time, I didn't know why the four of us, Dr. Livings and professor The Brand there were asleep. Indeed, regarding my Vigil, there are two different theories, but there in the talk for now bore.

Tempest and Heart-Sun hooded man approached. Tempest said: "We will not kill Dr. Livings ..."

"... And even Dr. Ivanovo", added Heart-Sun.

"That stupid that you are ... you can't stop. I have studied carefully, in recent months. I know the nicknames that you have data. Tempest, his time will be stopped!"

Tempest, in fact, stopped moving. I was thrilled. Tempest was K.O.! May not be able to escape? It was the turn of

Heart-Sun. He threw himself against the man hooded, but fell to the ground. Then the man took off the hood, and I pointed a finger, saying: "Now you know who I am. I'll have to kill her, Mr. JLH. I do not understand why it is still standing, but now it will be his turn".

I was even more horrified when I felt grab, and I found myself in another place. I was on the Grand Canyon, and by my side there was the Doctor! I looked. I was speechless.

The Doctor explained to me that this man had a hooded power: let people sleep, but had not noticed that she had managed to escape from his clutches. I asked: "And how do you stop the time individuals?"

"It's not him, but professor The Brand. We have been cheated. I, Heart-Sun and Tempest have been used for months by a criminal organization. I came back in time to block it. Something has gone awry: they managed to intercept me sooner than expected, and they changed the future. I today I would have had to find here. With my death, I would have blocked their powers, but unfortunately, to save you, there are successful. Could I ask you to put me to death instantly, but it's impossible. I have to save my friends, and then, you, as you are backing home?"

In fact, the Doctor left me there, explaining that this day would not have rained. How nice, I under the scorching sun, without a drop shadow ... but for the sake of mankind could even sacrifice.

When the Doctor returned to the University, the Rector, professor The Brand and Dr. Livings were ready to fulfill their criminal act: photographing everyone present, namely a strong layer of scientists, journalists, students, and others. They used a special camera, which uses a laser similar to that of "Genetic Scanner". They wanted everyone's DNA, and then create the clones that obey their will, eliminating the originals! The Doctor was back in time to prevent this to happen. This would change the fate of mankind! The Doctor used the "G.S. Revision 3.0" to read the DNA of three enemies. She began by professor The Brand. Shot him, then moved into space, he injected the DNA of Professor, and returned. She stopped time to each of the three. He then injected the DNA of the other two, and thus was able to wake up the people who dismiss. She did wake up even Heart-Sun and Tempest.

More time passed, and the Doctor became weak. So the three thugs awoke and gave lied. Neither trio knew how to lead the battle. After the escape of the three, Tempest I came to retrieve.

Chapter XIV

When I told what had happened, I asked: is it a dream?

The Doctor replied: "Good question. You are the only one that Incubus has not been able to sleep!"

"Incubus?" we went out in chorus.

"Yes," said the Doctor, "the Rector calls himself Incubus, professor The Brand does not chose any heroic name, while Dr. Livings, do you call Legend. Surely you will want to know their powers more fully. Incubus can make people fall asleep on command. The Brand freeze time individuals. Legend seems like writing telepathy with whoever is in front of him, and therefore able to tell about the time legends relating to ancestors of the people you comes in contact".

"Three weapons seem to be symbiotic. But tell me, because I don't fell asleep?"

"Maybe Incubus decided that you just stayed awake. On the other hand the fact that they decided to kill you would indicate that you are immune from attack. Tell me, do you suffer from insomnia?"

"Yes, even 10 gallons of Chamomile manage to make me fall asleep!"

"This explains why. You are stronger than him. The other two, however, are quite capable of using their power over you".

Tempest asked, "How do you explain that The Brand has managed to stop my?"

"I guess if you had learned of its power in advance, you'd be able to navigate through, as we are able."

"In fact", so I spoke, "you have placed in yourself the powers of Tempest and others?"

"No, actually, I already have the power to move through time and space. The day I tested the DNA of Tempest, and the memories you burned, in fact, was a travesty. The DNA of four Gig memories was my, DNA of the future, with all the powers that I have recovered from the DNA of others".

"What Is That? Now I look like a monster!" exclaimed Heart-Sun.

"I have the innate ability to read people's DNA being beside me, provided however that it is non-standard type, i.e. containing the information of the superpowers. That's why I don't read the DNA of JLH. This also allows me to know if non-standard DNA of another person is compatible with other DNA. Unfortunately, few people DNA allows non-standard additions. So far, only my DNA has proved compatible with all DNA. The "Genetic"

Scanner designed to read and transfer the DNA in others, but only I am able to decrypt without the aid of a super computer".

"I'm lost already at the beginning" severed Heart-Sun. "In any case, one thing is clear to me: I do not use that darn thing, I already have too many strange abilities".

Tempest said: "Now, you have the powers of all of them, right?"

"Yes, except that in me The Brand's powers don't seem to work properly. Do not last long because with him".

I caught the word: "I have a theory. They have developed a camera that can read DNA as Genetic Scanner, right? May have injected some sort of virus that does not allow the correct reading of their DNA?"

"It's a nice hypothesis. I'll have to check out my new DNA through the Scanner. Then will read through your PC, with your help, Heart-Sun. I had never met a virus of the genus".

Heart-Sun responded: "I, at this point, I would consider it more like a computer virus. Maybe we will with an antivirus".

After scanning the DNA doctor, I used an antivirus on the genetic code. He tracked down the virus. This virus was a binary code posted in the genetic code. It was an alteration of the basic three-digit code, which is the interpretation of DNA. Deleted the virus, the Doctor noticed that together we eliminated duplicate powers from Legend and Incubus. The Doctor asked me to act as Guinea pig, and I managed to successfully operate the power to stop my time.

When I recovered, I felt Tempest ask: "How Come I, despite being back in time on a mission, I don't remember anything about everything that concerns you, doctor?"

"Actually, you don't have to know anything! You had to go back to-back in time on your own, without knowing that I had the same power and had received the same position".

Heart-Sun stopped immediately: "Sorry, but still I am not clear one thing. Who we instructed to start a mission?".

Tempest said: "Eh! Eh! Would you like to know, is it? But, it's better that I don't say anything".

"Tempest, not treat it so. Declare him the truth".

"I don't want then mounts her head".

"We don't have to tell him all the details ... so ... the assignment came from the top chief in charge, namely you. With time, you'll start to lead our team. JLH will put in writing everything ourselves, creating a kind of diary.

By the way, the other day I sent me an invitation to come to us, JLH, because my joining in our team".

"And how will the chief? Between how long will happen? How many women I have around me? I don't I'll wife Doctor? No, I don't think, otherwise you rule together with me, instead, in a team, it takes only one chief, who knows how to get respect!"

"Since I told you? Now he has mounted his head! Not the end anymore!"

The Doctor replied: "Just as well. You can add more. You have to build it yourself your future. If you want, you can change it, and decide to decline the post of head".

"Yes, so you will continue to lead us around the Club's only female?"

I replied: "Is this the way to treat a lady?"

"Why, you married? Wait, while you are gone on the Grand Canyon, you made the statement ... you put on your knees, and you said that you love ... and you said yes?"

Tempest interjected: "You realize that we're fighting? Rather than thinking about the future captain of our team, let's figure out what to do to block those three!"

Tempest was speechless us all. We had to create a perfect plan to stop those criminally insane. How? Their powers in our comparison, rather than those of my friends, from a certain point of view they were equivalent.

We decided to return each at home, and spend the night to sleep on it. We counted on the fact that even his enemies would have acted similarly.

Arrived the next morning, and Heart-Sun was eager to communicate a fact strange. The previous night, had had a strange dream. Before starting the Doctor wanted to report her dream!

Heart-Sun began. Here is his story:

Chapter XV

Last night when I got home, I took a cold shower. Then I'm lying. At one point, I woke up to start, because I had seemed to have heard a noise. Being on those who go there, I stood up in haste. It seemed all right, and I went back to bed.

After I fell asleep, I started dreaming one thing strange. I saw a man, who lived in Sardinia, in the town of Bosa. He worked at the port. Her name was Antonio Soli'nas. The documents with which trafficked, I noticed that it was 1600! Dreaming, I traveled over time, how nice!

This man was devoted to trade with the Spaniards, who had just conquered Sardinia. I saw this man he took from a box a strange object. Took it home, and his wife, not knowing what it was, we put inside the Earth with one seed. From that seed grew a flower beautiful. The man put that strange "vase" in plain sight. Anyone who went to his house was left ecstatic. What I wanted to know what it was! I thought I couldn't communicate with him, but I couldn't even tell if they really exist!

Soli'nas brought that subject with him at work. Put it in plain sight on the table on which he worked. When people passed and saw that object, was left open-mouthed. Over time, they began to say to him: 'What good you were! You turned a rhino horn in planter!' And then it was dubbed *Su Corru*, meaning "Horn".

At that point, the man was gazing towards my direction (yet still didn't understand if I was there as a person, or simply I was observing from a distance). I pointed my finger, and I said: 'You're a horn! You are a descendant of mine! You have to unify my family! You must delete the rot that there is in the world!'

Immediately after I woke up, and it seemed to me as seeing a shadow leaving my room. This dream seems to explain my roots, my origins! My Russian surname, in fact, would be born in Sardinia?

JLH, what do you think?

"I already knew this legend. You just told the story of my family! It is said that my surname is born that's right! Do you want to see that we are relatives?"

The Doctor commented: "It seems that there is a close connection between all of us! I can't read your DNA, JLH, but I can try it with your Scanner, and then do a comparison with Heart-Sun. In any case, if you remember, Legend told me a similar story, when we met for the first time. And don't forget that even Tempest belongs to a lineage that is called Klein Horn, meaning 'Little Horn', in German. I would add that each of you has the same name, though in English, Russian and German. And my last name appears to be a diminutive form of your name. Are coincidences? I don't think. Perhaps, we are victims, in fact, descendants of a larger design. The noises that you hear at night and shadows that did leave were Incubus and Legend. Incubus made you fall asleep, and dream of a Legend connected with the past of your family".

This was the night that changed our lives.

Chapter XVI

Now it's time that I tell my dream. I am afraid that after I fell asleep, Incubus and Legend have managed to penetrate into my house.

My dream was even weirder. I saw an unusual baby, monstrous. It had two heads, four arms and two legs; In short, it was about two conjoined twins, opposite sex. They were just born. Doctors were deciding whether to be operated and divided. They didn't know if they would be able to save them.

The surgeon must perform the operation touched the twin's head, and said: 'This kid is really dashing! Has the hot-headed, but doesn't seem to have a fever. His heart is beating very strong'.

Then he touched the head of mate, and soon after began to smile. He said satisfied tone: 'We can operate. I'm sure the two children will be healthy'.

I saw then operate and divide the two children. The operation succeeded perfectly.

I wanted to tell you about this dream so much, because I believe that Legend has managed to make me dream an incident linked to my past. You and me, Heart-Sun, we are brothers! We are Siamese twins!

"What? You and me ...? No, you can't!"

Instead, it is so; now we had to investigate, to research. Heart-Sun began to consult the databases electronically. Tempest, however, had the idea of time travel, and precisely to go to discover who the surgeon who performed the operation was. He made an amazing discovery. He saw his father he touched the two heads. When he touched the head of mate, the two traveled in time for a brief moment.

Tempest returned in our time, and described what he saw. The Doctor said: "Now I understand why I could pass my power in you, no problems! The power was born probably in the time when thou hast touched! Maybe your power has remained hidden until the day that we met up with your old father!"

"But one thing I don't understand: my dad is a famous musician, not a surgeon!"

"We are talking with them now. Do come here".

Tempest immediately tried to track down his father. It was not traceable. He had disappeared. The housekeeper told him: "He disappeared about two days ago. Did not leave say in what place was, but I think that it was engaged in a scientific conference".

Tempest realizes that his father wanted to participate at the Conference of Dr. Livings. On the other hand had not been among those present! He decided to try to move to his father, to find out what she had done.

When he arrived, he was tied to a Chair. It was in a dark place. A few moments later he heard: "Finally arrived, Mr. Tempest. We were waiting for her. We skip the pleasantries, so we know each other already, remember?"

"She is Legend? She has kidnapped my father!"

"Yes, it's true. We were sure that she came to her rescue".

"You don't have kept in mind that I can leave whenever I want".

"Yes, but if she were to leave, it could become an orphan".

"OK. You want from me?".

"We want to simply retrieve its DNA, and then get rid of her."

"But I can handle this power".

"We don't know; that's why it will kill the now".

Tempest attempted to free them, but the ropes were harsh. He knew that even if he had moved in space, it would be found once again tied. He was about to move to a place far away, when he began to think: 'If I escape, my family will always be in danger. It is better that I study their moves: perhaps I will understand how to address them and defeat them. ... If only I could warn my buddies ...'

When The Brand was going to scan it with the camera, the room began to move. A few moments later, the wall began to crumble. Heart-Sun and the Doctor had arrived. The three foes tried to block them with their powers, but the Doctor had succeeded meanwhile studying their DNA, despite the virus, and figure out how to avoid being blocked. It had provided Heart-Sun and JLH a special clock with different capacities. More on that later, otherwise we lose too much time and here there is Tempest to save!

The Doctor ran towards Tempest, which emerged. Heart-Sun put between each other and enemies. Tempest arose, touched the two companions and returned together with them in the lab.

There, he received his watch. This watch was able to repel the attacks of The Brand, but it was also equipped with transceiver and GPS radar.

In the laboratory now there were Grandfather Klein and Dr. Klein. Tempest returned to be the doctor. So, they could finally turn to Grandfather Klein, and hope to find different answers.

The Doctor asked him: "Mr. Klein, she once was a surgeon, right?"

"I was in another life. I was younger".

"25 years ago, definitely," said Heart-Sun. "Me and the Doctor we have twenty-five years. And now she has divided us twenty-five years ago".

"Yes, it's true. It is right that we explain several things. Twenty-five years ago I was a surgeon. Yours was the last operation. That day I got home, I sat near the piano at home had the simple role of being in plain sight. Without knowing why I started to play, and discovered to be able! A few minutes later I heard ringing the Bell. It was a neighbor. I thought of having disturbed, instead, I presented a host, a famous conductor. And so it was that I left the surgery for the piano".

"Interesting, but why not, Daddy, did you start from the beginning?"

"Oh! Sorry kids. OK, I started directly after the conclusion. It was the summer of 1980. For months we studied how to act in your comparisons. You were born attached, 29 January. For nearly eight months, I and many other experts were discussing on how to act, when in late August started to sick. You were almost in a coma. We did bring in surgical room quickly. Your parents were warned that in all likelihood one of you would be dead. We had to decide who was the healthiest, and sacrificing the other twin. The decision was very difficult: to me it was the last word. I decided to choose, caressing your heads. The cutest face you would be saved. This was the hardest of decisions: I know that after that day, I would have retired. It was a burden too great to decide the fate of others, especially when it came to two children. When I touched your head, Heart-Sun, I felt a strange feeling. You came out strange warmth out of normal, yet you had no fever. You were sweaty, but your sweat droplets were ice cold. I sacrifice you..."

"Let Alone. The lovely Mary is saved, and the ugly Joann died! I was born just unlucky!"

"Yes, and you're still alive!" said the Doctor. "Let's continue the story to Mr. Klein".

"Well, where I was left? Yes, I touched your head, Mary, and a strange light blinded me for a moment. When I reactivated my eyes, I was at home, but I was a kid. I looked in the mirror: I was my grandson, and I was in your company! Then I accompanied you, Mary, at home. I think you remember that occasion, it was the day in which you all but Mr. JLH, you know. Then I went back to my time, and I realized that I could operate without problems: you saved both. It took nearly two years to plan the operation".

"Is a chilling story, dad. That day, so no I brought my son, but you with me?"

"No, I have appeared here at the University. Your son was here with you".

Heart-Sun, who seemed a little face stunned, interjected: "Well, now I have a serious question. Who are our real parents?"

"Good question, my son. You should know that after the operation, your parents weren't there anymore. I undertake an investigation by a group of Italian investigators. Discover that your mother, alas, had died in give you the light, and that your father was a Soviet spy. You were the result of an experiment. They found the documents, which, however, were not written in Russian, but in German. It seems that you have been the result of a Nazi project, dating back 40 years earlier! Your father had managed to retrieve the documents and, as a reward, the KGB decided to experiment with the design on your mother. Sometime later, your father was put to death. By contrast, years later, I heard your father speak again: it was said that he was alive, and that he had fled from the Soviet Union with his daughter. Unfortunately, I never had concrete confirmation. However, the two that I had brought to the hospital and disappeared, we decided to entrust you, Mary, a French-Italian couple, Alex Innoce'nti and Anne Petite. You, Joann, were entrusted to a Russian family, the Rajok".

The Doctor asked: "Wherefore, our father might still be alive? What is your name?"

"Your father's name was Alexander Ivanovo. If I understand correctly, isn't really dead, and seems to have managed to find you, Mary".

"No, the Alexander Ivanovo he heard is, in fact, the man to whom he entrusted me, Alex Innoce'nti. He had decided to change its name when I was a child, and began calling himself Alexander Ivanovo".

Heart-Sun intervened: "That's great! Thus, even if adopted, you've got the surname of our father. I've always been Rajok. The usual fortune ..."

"Who was the couple who took us to the hospital, so?" asked the Doctor.

"Good question. They came as Peter and Anne Grant".

"Hey! Are my uncles! Anne is our father's sister!".

"How?"

"Yes, Uncle Peter is a surgeon, and her aunt Anne is a great pianist".

"I was a surgeon, and the last time I saw them, I became a pianist!"

The Doctor replied: "I have a theory. Probably the aunt's DNA is not standard. I have always had a special relationship with her. Next to her, I always felt as ready for the future and especially sure of me. Now I understand: you are able to pass on their powers in others. I think that to repay her, has given this ability".

"Your uncle was a surgeon? In any case, not working in my own hospital, but I knew that finding the right parents whose trust, had occupied a doctor in another hospital, wanted to remain anonymous".

"Therefore, in summary, my uncles should not be my real uncles, because I would have been adopted, and my stepfather would mock the brother of my sister's real father. As a result, my uncles are really my uncles! Now only remains for me a question: my stepmother Anne was Petite. It's actually existed?"

Grandfather Klein replied: "There's still something you have to clarify: our surnames. Unfortunately, I don't know all the details, but as you may have guessed by now, are always the same, which are repeated in all languages. 'Klein' is German, 'Petite' is French, and has the same meaning. 'Ivanovo' derives from 'Ivan', variant of Russian name 'Joann'. Once again, we note the repetition of a name, in different languages".

JLH intervened: "I understand that there I enter in this game of names".

"Yes, it is so. I believe that we have some common ancestry. I think we should go around 1600".

The Doctor said: "Remember that I wanted to compare the DNA of JLH and Heart-Sun? However, I think if we compare to each of us, we'd find out they are related. Meanwhile, here are the results of the comparison of JLH and Heart-Sun. Yes, there are many similar traits, especially those standards. They are nearly identical. There are no relevant differences, respect the comparison between people whose ancestors date back to the time of the Deluge".

Chapter XVII

As you know, I don't really like writing, but now I want to tell you firsthand the journey that I decided to undertake. It would allow knowing the origins of our family, and maybe how to defeat our enemies once and for all.

I suggested to my friends to come with me in the 17th century. No matter how tempting, noted that it would have been dangerous: If we ended up in an era where there was only one of our ancestors, we didn't know it would happen. So I traveled alone.

I wound in the body of Mr. Soli'nas, the same as the dream of Heart-Sun. After a few moments, however, I found to be his nephew. I couldn't stay at that time. I tried to be his father, but even in that era. It seems that for a period of almost a hundred years I possibly could be. It is as if there is a temporal shield. I tried to go at the time of his grandfather by Soli'nas, and we succeeded. According to the Doctor, this time it happened something so important, that I am not given to change history.

Thus, traveling in two eras, namely in the previous and in the next one to Soli'nas, I managed to discover various things. In the following lines, you will discover, as they will reveal.

Soli'nas was really a trader. He specialized in commercial exchange paying with salt. His right arm was nicknamed Sala'ris. Trading with the Spanish, in addition to receiving the famous Horn, hence the surname, also received a document. It was a map, indicating important information. What, however, is not known (?). The map is said to be disappearing by the time I arrived. According to the Doctor, that document is so important, that should belong only to its time. In my opinion, however, is so important, that contains the answer to the facts of the time when you are reading this book.

As you may recall I had to return the dress with H. G. Wells. Well, when I found myself at a time of deadlock, I decided to go find it. For some reason, though, missed my coordinates, and I found myself in another place: I was in the body of a man who was marrying a woman, a certain *Re* (Italian; "King" in English). After I transferred into the body of a Tempest, reported the dress to the rightful owner.

I decided to travel back in time to discover the origins of the Re family. I found myself in a strange time. I was sitting on a throne. It didn't take me long to realize that I was a King! And who was I? Charlemagne!

The year was 774. Catalonia had just been conquered, so I'd just realized, when I was transferred to a later, the famous Christmas Eve, one where I was, hem, pardon, Charlemagne was crowned by Pope Leo III. Of course, I left, and I expressed my Crown that was born the Holy Roman Empire. A few days later, I found myself with a general talk. He had a document in his hand. He explained that he had been found in Catalonia, a Roman site. As I touched it, I found myself beaten again from that era to the 21st century, to the present time in which this book was written. I tried to go back to the 19th century, but once again seemed to have lifted a temporal shield.

I decided to work around, going to Roman times when it was written the document. This required a great concentration, because I didn't know what was at the time, and I had to be careful not to end up in the wrong place!

When I finished the journey, I felt someone calling: "*Ave, Caesar!*" Yes, I was Gaius Julius Caesar (Latin, *Gaius Iulius Caesar*)! It didn't take me long to realize that I was dealing with Brutus (*Marcus Junius Brutus Caepio*). I was naturally telling him: "We will meet again at Philippi". He looked at me in a weird way. He had in his hand a scroll. I said: "Behold the parchment if you required. I need to dictate something?"

I answered: "No, for now can suffice. Leave me here, which I'll write sheet a private document. Leave me alone".

It seems that I had arrived at the time when it was written that document. A question I clutched him: 'I would have been sent back to another era?' On the other hand, did not know about the content of the document, and therefore what I could write? I decided to try to write a message. As I touched the sheet, I was hurled into another era. It was 15 March 44. Before me, there were several men. Brutus had in hand the parchment, and together with others was ready to stab me. Not to change the story, immediately I told him: "*Kai su, teknon*" ("You too, my son?")? I realized, of telling him the phrase in Greek, self-cheating, and immediately I said in Latin: "*Tu quoque, Brute, fili mi!*" Feeling the forces failed, I thought that was the end, but was slammed back into the 21st century. I was alive, but no document. When I told him what had happened, the Doctor made me notice that the story has it that Caesar, before venting the last breath, spoke to Brutus in Greek, not Latin.

Who knows, maybe I had changed the story? Maybe now it would become possible to retrieve that document, arriving at times of Soli'nas or Charlemagne. ... Nothing to do was still standing temporal shield.

Chapter XVIII

We were there for the vanquished, when, in the laboratory, came a young schoolgirl, begging to speak privately with Professor Ivanovo. Mary explained that the time available was little, but insisted that she needed to solve a problem. Here are the facts of the day.

"Good morning, Professor Ivanovo".

"Good morning, Miss Kaiser. The warn you: today I don't have much time".

"I was hoping that I was paying a few moments: only you can help me solve my problem".

Mary had headaches to solve: getting rid of three dangerous men, equipped with non-standard DNA and figure out how to reach a document "elusive". He had already decided not to pay attention to the girl, when he thought: 'Maybe a moment of distraction will do me just fine'.

"Miss, either. If I can, I will".

"Thank you very much! We can talk in private?"

"Agree … we leave them alone for a few minutes? … Thank You".

"Professor, I know she is considered the most knowledgeable in the world when it comes to deciphering the genetic code ... behold, I need you to help me understand if I am sick, if I'm dying!"

"Why do you say so?"

"For some time now I have strange disorders".

"How Come you are not directed to a doctor?"

"I do not feel. It is as if something brings me to go to her. It is as if there was no other solution, if you don't ask her the solution".

'How strange ... but quirks in these times ...' he thought the Doctor.

"Let's see what we can do," said the Doctor, who now had an antinomy: use Genetic Scanner or examine your blood? He chose the blood test. As she touched the girl's arm, he noticed that something was amiss. It began to look at her in a strange way. Yes, Ms. Katia Kaiser had a non-standard DNA. However why the Doctor had not noticed before? Probably because, as it turned out, was still unstable this DNA.

The Doctor began to realize that the girl had developed natural capacities so superior to the majority of human beings. However, he did not report it at once to Katia; first needed to understand which side they would be deployed. So did the simple blood test.

"Ms. Kaiser, I wish I was going to take in the University Library of some books. Now I write the titles on a sheet. These books will interpret what is reported in the outcome of the examination".

While Katia went to the library, the Doctor called JLH and Heart-Sun to mention something. He explained that he had given a first test, but hoped that Heart-Sun could entrust other "assignments". Did in time to finish this meeting, that Katia was immediately returned. It had brought books. The Doctor told her:

"As I told Miss, I'm very busy. My colleagues, you see, are indented; we have to resume our work. I invite you to watch the results, and to look for the data in the books that I did pick. If you can find alone the outcome, it will have a good vote".

Katia didn't understand, but looking at the paper, began to "Browse" books. Within a few seconds were all useful pages for analysis. We announced: "Books, it seems that I'm in perfect health".

"As promised, give a good rated".

"She knew that I was right?"

"Yes, even before the examination. I wanted to test".

"Put me to the test?"

"Yes. She was able to read the results of his blood test at the same speed reached by me, with a difference: she needed some books".

Heart-Sun intervened: "Well done the sister. It's always the bigger!"

"You seem a way to offend a girlfriend, Joann?" replied the Doctor.

"Ah! Forgive me!"

Katia said: "I'm not seeing much".

"Let's see how to help her," replied the Doctor. "So, take in hand this newspaper. Go to the quizzes page. You start to solve the exercises".

Once you have finished the exercises, the Doctor continued: "You know how long it takes to solve the exercises? About five minutes".

"Are joking? I spent over an hour!"

"No, she took about five minutes. My colleagues can confirm".

"I've never spent five minutes to solve many puzzle exercises. Anyway, I notice that I've solved all these exercises, and some definitions related to concepts that I had never studied before! ... I am getting more confused".

"Now I will try to explain them that happen. When she must decipher something, time slows down for you. Nobody around notice: it seems that all is always at the same speed".

"No? And it can be shown with a stopwatch?"

"Yes. Take this stopwatch: The lean, where he wants, in a place that is not visible to us. So we cannot tamper with. Then start looking for *Genetics for everyone — New and old theories: a journey through time and into the human body*. Meanwhile the clock controls which are on her wrist".

When Katia returned, was appalled! "According to the clock on my wrist, I would have taken about three minutes to track down the book. According to the timer which I started, however, I spent less than three seconds! I am always confused. It seems that time for me walk differently, right? ..."

The Doctor added: "... I'd say unstable. At certain times for her time speeds up, slows down, and according to need. That's why lately felt strange".

"Still not clear me one thing. How is it possible that I have managed to solve the entire exercises puzzle?"

"Quite simply, she is a decipherer. She is able to decipher anything. She slows down time, so is able to decipher a puzzle in a few seconds, though for her this can take hours".

"I understand … One last question: when I slow down the tempo, get older?"

"Good question. Joann, what do you think?"

"Ahem! Beauty does not arise from today to tomorrow", said Heart-Sun.

"I don't understand!" asked Katia.

"I think my brother would say: 'The beauty does not change from one day to the next'. It means that while being passed by her, Miss, hours, when she came back from us, was always the same. Probably his body follows the normal aging. His DNA is able to adjust too. It's just lucky!"

Heart-Sun now said, seriously: "Miss, I would like to ask one thing".

The Doctor interjected: "Be careful what you say, brother! Avoid saying some howler!"

"Don't worry sister!" Then turned to Katia: "We have made a solemn Pact, namely to protect humanity from someone who has a non-standard DNA, and use their specially developed faculties to hurt …" The Doctor began to think: '… That serious and profound discourse! …'

"…How to use his abilities?"

"It's already so if I start to understand something. I would not have this weight on my body. For now, I hope to learn to control my skills and maybe, one day may be used to assist and protect humanity".

"If this day had already arrived?" asked JLH.

"Help me learn to control myself from now!"

Heart-Sun said: "Alright, you now enter the Universal Club! How can we call it?"

Each proposed a name. Thinking of the surname, the Doctor said: "Caesarian".

JLH suggested: "Small Storm".

Dr. Klein: "Rebus".

Heart-Sun agreed that it was called "Rebus", but Katia replied: "In Russia 'Hero' they say *ghieroi* [герой]. Therefore, I would like to be called Gilroy Bury [Буря Герой, 'Storm Hero']".

Really, it would be more correct to call it Герой Бури, "Hero of the Tempest", but chose her, and they all agree.

Chapter XIX

He explained to Gilroy Bury, the particular situation in which he found the Club. In particular, it explained the fact untraceable document. Meanwhile, she offered to help solve the headache, Tempest appeared, accompanied by a boy.

"Hello, I present to you Moradh Lifneh. Coming from Israel, and has twenty-two years. Its name means 'Against Rebellion'. I traveled for the time, trying to find the key to reaching that famous document. Finally, I suggested that a decipherer would do to our case. I opted for a Canaanite, direct descendant of one of the architects of the famous 'Tower of Babel'. Doctor, I think I will confirm that his DNA is non-standard. In fact, he has an innate ability to speak any language. I nicknamed Poliglottix".

"Yes, I confirm. His DNA is non-standard. Anyway, we had already found a decipherer! ... Meet Katie Kaiser, aka Gilroy Bury".

Gilroy Bury replied: "I'm glad to finally know the great Tempest! ... I'll be happy to work with you, Poliglottix".

Poliglottix said: "Thank you very much for your welcome. Tempest told me everything. Whenever I have to exchange information of any kind, through voice, writing, or signs, with people of any language, I naturally respond".

Heart-Sun interjected: "Alright, alright. I'm glad to know that a new Member has joined the Club. Give us a hand definitely in the fight against the bad guys".

Poliglottix replied: "OK, Boss! But, tell me about these bad".

Gilroy Bury asked: "Before, why don't you tell us about yourself? How did you discover your power? How have you been approached by Tempest? So, who are you?"

Heart-Sun interrupted: "How is it? You're already in love with him?"

Tempest said: "Joann, you're always usually".

Poliglottix broke off the discussion: "Now, as you said Tempest, I come from Israel. For too long this country is terrifying upheaval theatre. About ten years ago I found myself involved in a battle near a lake. There were people from different African ethnic groups, when suddenly she heard one of them speaking in a strange language. After a few minutes, I noticed that was telling in a language they did not know about the name, which centuries ago was built the famous Tower of Babel because of which we descended all with different languages. This entry then said to me: 'Get up, you don't do anything'. Then I offered to drink from his water bottle. I was walking lamely; I hurt, and so helped me reach a calmer place. I cured wounds, and allowed me to have saves lives. The place where I brought was a field hospital, where he brought other people injured in the clash. There were Africans, Europeans and Americans, all under the care of a medical team that seemed to have no trouble taking care. What surprised me was that I was able to understand anyone who spoke to me, in your own language! I, on the other hand, in replying I was talking senselessly in all world languages. Many thought that same raving; it took a long time before I understood that my brain had started to develop thoughts in different languages ".

Gilroy Bury asked: "And the person, who saved you, who was it?"

"I don't know. Do not tell me her name. It went away right away".

The Doctor asked: "And how did you meet you and Tempest?"

Tempest took the floor: "I'll explain myself. The Tower of Babel was demolished around 130 years after the flood. However, I have not been able to reach that age, perhaps because too important to human history. I was born in a later, approximately 200 years later. I met Sharkalisharri, King of Agade (Akkad). He explained to me how at Babylon restored a Templar Tower, which existed from at least two centuries. A curiosity: as you know, when time travel, I speak the language of the ancestor that played; with Sharkalisharri I thought that I would need an interpreter, since my ancestor was not an Acadian, from family Japhetic, but a descendant of Javan, father of Elishah. Well, Sharkalisharri I replied in my language. I noticed then that he spoke other languages. In addition, near his throne there was a tiger. They communicate with each other, in the "language" of the Tigers! Including therefore that it was not simple study of any language, but an innate ability to understand and speak any language! So, I was sure of having found the person I was looking for. Now I had to follow the timeline of his offspring, and hope that we had come. Even if the person that I found had not been equipped with this power, I was sure it was concealed in his DNA. In fact, almost all descendants of Sharkalisharri proved to be free of this power. Fortunately, our Moradh Lifneh was not lacking!"

At this point, our friends explained to Poliglottix of our enemies Incubus, Legend and The Brand, which you know well; therefore you don't need to read this dialogue.

Chapter XX

Yesterday he came back from his trip temporal Tempest. This morning our friends are indented in the University laboratory. Poliglottix obviously came first, because others have got together, and he was on the phone. Of course, nobody asked him anything.

It's finally time to make stock of the situation. The Club now has six elements. The Club has three enemies. We seem to benefit. Their powers are difficult to defeat. It seems that the only solution is to track down the famous document that has appeared several times over the past 2,000 years.

At the moment we know that has been compiled by Julius Caesar some time before his death. Her son Brutus took it into custody. The paper then was found in a cave in Spain about the time when Charlemagne was crowned King of the Holy Roman Empire. In 1600 that document had passed into the hands of the Aragonese, and then flew to Sardinia. After that, we couldn't find any trace of that sheet.

We also know that, usually, passed through the hands of the descendants of Tempest, JLH, the Doctor and Heart-Sun. You might assume, therefore, that they should once again be the receivers of the document.

Gilroy Bury has just finished putting together the pieces of the puzzle. "It lacks at least one piece!" exclaimed. "I have given all details".

The Doctor commented: "It seems that we just found out your weak point, Gilroy Bury. You develop so quickly, but you need to have complete data. ... We need to understand what you don't have".

Heart-Sun intervened: "We know that the document in one way or another is always passed into the hands of some of our ancestor. Tempest, remember that time you've found in the life of your direct ancestor, but into that of an Italian?" This is so far the only case in which Tempest you is found in a man, but a woman.

"Yes ...".

"Stop all, I understand what you mean, Heart-Sun" severed Gilroy Bury. "You, Tempest, were brought into the Church where he had kept the document! Where?"

"Unfortunately, I don't know. There I stayed for a long time. I think though that I would be able to recognize it if I saw it again".

The Doctor said: "Perhaps Gilroy Bury can do a search in the library, and JLH and Heart-Sun on the Internet?"

After a while, JLH presented research report: "I think it is the Putifigari Church (SS)".

Tempest and Gilroy Bury there went immediately. Using the Super-speed, Gilroy Bury analyzed the entire religious venue. He found that the document had been found in the tomb of Antonio Escaneo, a priest. After a restore, the document had disappeared.

When he finished his investigation, lasting a few seconds, Gilroy Bury realized that Tempest had disappeared, and that some people were watching the sky. The felt exclaim: "…Yet the sky is clear! It doesn't seem that you are approaching a thunderstorm". This had understood that people had heard the thunder of Tempest, which walked away from there, moving in space.

He had to use his Super-speed to return to college soon. The Super-speed also allowed them to run on water. When he entered the lab, she immediately realized that there was neither Tempest, nor Klein.

While referring to the Doctor of his discoveries, the boys went looking for Tempest. JLH and Heart-Sun in particular began to search for information on the Internet. They took us all over the world. Poliglottix, instead, used the phone. He phoned authorities from around the world. Nevertheless Tempest seemed to have pulverized. They were unable to contact either with Klein's grandfather, son, and grandson. It was as if an entire genealogical line had disappeared.

Gilroy Bury suddenly exclaimed: "I know what happened! You can't have four contacts with the document. Although in that Church was gone, the physique of Tempest has warned perhaps the remains. In fact, under the heel of my shoe I just found a piece of paper. Looks like a piece of paper. I'm afraid I too approached Tempest during the search, and that therefore he was banged in another place, perhaps far away. It is likely that you have been transported the entire 'Tempest'".

The Doctor took the gloves and took the piece of paper. All feared the worst, but nothing happened. By Carbon 14 analysis, the Doctor was able to deduce that that piece of paper said to a little over 2,000 years ago. There is a symbol, an effigy, with two initials in a semicircle: **D I** which means DIVVS IVLIVS. Under the image there was an inscription in ancient Greek, Καίσαρ (*Kaisar*, or "Kaiser") and a drawing of a Greek temple, identical to the Putifigari Church but also at the entrance of the University!

Poliglottix now a matter remarked: "I know that you are excited by the findings, but I would point out that this document to you three, Doctor, Heart-Sun and JLH, could prove to be dangerous, because it has already put in KO Tempest and family".

Gilroy Bury added: "Yes, I was thinking too. I don't know at this point whether it is really the key to defeat enemies, or rather to be defeated!"

The Doctor replied: "I think this document is like the poison of snakes. The antidote lies in the venom itself. Anyway, in my analysis of the document, I checked the DNA. I made an amazing discovery: the genetic code of this Papyrus sheet contains all the information of my powers, Heart-Sun, Tempest, and at least one other person ..."

"Another person?" severed Heart-Sun. "And so there would be another 'Little Horn'? This time he where would arrive from China?"

The Doctor replied: "Before we describe the power, then you will understand. This power is insomnia ".

JLH said: "Insomnia? ... I suffer insomnia, but you know very well that my DNA is standard type!"

"In fact, yours is a non-DNA-related insomnia. Looks like you have in your body a substance without DNA, which allows you to withstand Incubus. Let me analyze your blood, to learn more about this substance".

Chapter XXI

It is dark. Seem to hear more tunes move for this dark. It seems that there is someone. Some arms touching other bodies. Someone is breathing. Breaths intertwine, creating more types of airs. Someone is missing, but it's dark.

"Who is there? Where am I?" he felt a trembling voice startled me.

'He-he!' was rumored. Someone coughed.

"Daddy, where are you? Why is there cold? Why is there the dark? You can turn on the light?" roared up a child's voice.

"Are you, Vladimir, my son?"

"Yes, dad … why didn't turn on the light?"

"Excuse me; are the voices of Vladimir and Johannes, those that feel?"

"Yes," replied Johannes, "and you are my father, Wolfgang?"

"Yes. It's me, my sons".

There was a voice saying confusedly: "Where are we? Who am I? Because I am not one of you? By which time I come, I?"

Wolfgang said: "Thou art the true Tempest, isn't it? You need to have brought us here, for some reason ".

"No. Remember I was in Italy, Sardinia, helping Gilroy Bury, when I found myself catapulted here, suddenly". From the answers of the other three, it was clear that this had happened to all four simultaneously.

Wolfgang asked Tempest: "Did you ask 'Who are they? Where did I come from?' Why?"

"Why do I have a memory blank? I remember what I did when I swapped my DNA with your, but I don't remember anything".

Johannes interjected: "I remember what happened the day of the train wreck. Until that day you remembered that you were sent back in time to save the future. Therefore, you should remember what happened in your future, to know who you are".

Wolfgang, who was a surgeon, he said: "Maybe in the future there will be. Perhaps something has changed today our future. As a result, you will the world not Tempests. Perhaps you have been confined in our present, and can't remember your future, because it does not exist".

"If so, I'm supposed to disappear at any moment ..."

"The world around us has vanished. Why? There is nothing, no matter where I try to move," said the little Vladimir.

"Vladimir! My son, Vladimir, what you said is sad!" said Johannes.

Unfortunately, yes, it seems that the four were found in a time Vortex into a black hole, which would have eliminated their current and future genealogy. However, they are still alive! I'm not dead! Have not disappeared entirely! If I am able to report this event, meaning that they have never disappeared. I have communicated the facts, isn't it? Now you'll know what happened.

In the laboratory the University Doctor had analyzed the DNA of JLH. She had discovered that, in fact, had never been standard type. DNA has developed a protective shield, which prevented the Doctor understand that JLH has a non-standard DNA. Fine, but what has this to do with the four unlucky?

However, in the meantime, the two existing discovered that Julius Caesar was a secret document, of which the annals of time talking, but that it was not arrived at our days. In fact, a piece of that document had been found under the feet of Gilroy Bury. Thanks to a detailed analysis, it was discovered he was actually. From the village of Putifigari, it had been brought to Trento by a descendant of King who was getting married. It was analyzed the descent of woman, to find that a man during World War II he moved to Trento. He was a financier. There was much Gilroy understand that Bury the document could be in Command of local *Guardia di Finanza*. Gilroy Bury there went on a mission with Poliglottix.

The latter waited outside. Gilroy Bury entered surreptitiously. Thanks to its ability to Flex time moves faster than range of cameras, and hid some two-way radios inside the barracks. So, out, Poliglottix listened to conversations. In an Office, Gilroy Bury found a chest of drawers, with written "*Trènt und Trìent? DI*" ("Trent und Trent? DI"). Is curious: could be in one of those drawers? The drawers were sealed. We would have wanted the strength of Heart-Sun to open them. The girl could not speak, because it would otherwise have been discovered. So he had to leave in a hurry from the barracks, and approach the machine where expected Poliglottix to propose his plan to resolve the situation. It was almost a surprise to see his traveling companion on the phone. She asked him if he was on the phone with two teammates at the University. He replied no, but recalled that they had probably a long time. Thus, should speed up. It attempted to link the mobile to a rope whose other end was tied to the car. He had never tried to Flex time, where was not present. There would be managed? Poliglottix pressed on the accelerator, but the movement was causing too much noise. The girl was about to be discovered.

Meanwhile, unaware of what was happening, the Doctor and Heart-Sun made a shocking discovery. Meanwhile who put some order in the lab; they found strange photographs and documents.

The barracks door was open. The handle was already lowered. Gilroy Bury was seeking a solution in haste so as not to be discovered, and to tidy up the room. The door began to open up, and he felt a thud. She approached slowly and carefully at the door: three financiers were ashore. They were ... snoring comfortably. She turned around, and who saw? He saw three men. They offered to help her carry out her chest of drawers. Were the three worst enemies of the Club! After having untied the dresser, this was transported inside the barracks. Thanks to Super-speed of Gilroy Bury, they arrived at the car that was waiting outside. Gilroy Bury went with them.

On the other machine, Poliglottix saw everything. Immediately grabbed the phone, and felt Heart-Sun and the Doctor. The latter, meanwhile, had sensed that one of the last two members of the team was a spy. Photographs and documents found in the Office drove them to check your emails: in recent days, several e-mail exchanges between Gilroy Bury and Incubus! Enemies now had the key with him. How could they save Klein?

When Poliglottix returned, the team was particularly shaken by recent events. It seemed to have been dismembered slowly. As you may have noticed, in recent events, a member of the Club has not been included. Yes, JLH was absent to attend to some family chores. Now back to the University, where he asks his friends:

"What happened to Gilroy Bury? He texted me, saying: 'Have been discovered. I fear for what could happen'".

"We've been betrayed by Gilroy Bury. He handed the key to Caesar the enemy ..." replied the Doctor.

"... Now we kill, and conquer the world", added Heart-Sun

"A moment, the whole thing seems strange. Why we should betray?"

Poliglottix said: "Here's. It was introduced to the Club. Did he believe in need of help, but seemed to know from the outset of powers. We used".

JLH asked Hearts-Sun if they could talk in private. He asked why, the team was still together. In any case, agreed. JLH showed him other messages that did not want see Poliglottix.

The first said: "Poliglottix is always on the phone. I'm afraid that when I need him, will be distracted".

The second said: "The key is in a chest of very heavy and cannot be opened".

The third said: "We are striving to poach the dresser".

The fourth said: "They were enemies. I am flexing the time to write this message".

"Later, I've got other messages. I fear that has made Poliglottix capture and has stuck".

"How can we fail to see that there is cheating?" asked Heart-Sun. JLH proposed to do a test "telephonically".

When returned in the lab, Heart-Sun asked to borrow your phone to Poliglottix. These of course asked why. Heart-Sun responded that it's not working, for low battery. Poliglottix agreed. Heart-Sun joined the list of incoming calls and outgoing calls but found nothing. Gated section, but it was almost empty. The thing wasn't working. The Doctor had sensed something, so he said:

"You know, Poliglottix, that you were in Trento, I decided to find out who was the person who had saved his life. Having the ability to move in space, I went in search of the lake where the clash took place in which life you tested. I spoke with someone, and I discovered that the doctor who saved him was called Livings". Imagine how they felt others present. The goose was sleeping at all, and for different reasons! Poliglottix had been hired by Legend, and now formed part of the villains! These were framed for well Gilroy Bury. Now Poliglottix was forced to report where they held the girl. The methods of Heart-Sun were very convincing. The Doctor moved quickly through space, and arrived at the hideout. He grabbed the girl, who reported to the University, in haste.

"What did you do? Why I was released, without recovering documents?"

"I didn't know that they had opened the dresser! We make?"

She said: "We have to go, Doctor. Only we can retrieve the key. You can't go alone, because you cannot touch. I can't move through space like you".

The two women went. They discovered that they can join in. Changing the time, Gilroy Bury allowed the Doctor not to be discovered, but also to move simultaneously in time and space. Finally, when they returned to College, Gilroy could put hand to Bury document of Caesar, but not before receiving an excuse on the part of his teammates.

Poliglottix had been brought from Heart-Sun and JLH to police but thanks to the other three companions he was able to escape the prison.

Chapter XXII

Finally, Gilroy Bury could control the document, the key to free Klein. In all this, none of them knew that with the three Klein there was also a fourth man to be freed.

The document contained a strange speech in Latin, hard to decipher even for the largest decipher in the world, Katia Kaiser. Here is the text of the document:

Egomet, DI, Superi Infiniti Spatii et Temporis,

Vaco, vaco tempo et invenio.

Detineo tempus.

Agglutino et conglutino Solis et pluviae.

Muto.

Detineo tempus.

Detineo tempus.

Detineo tempus et spatii et pluviae.

Detineo tempus.

Minime dormio.

Here's the translation of Gilroy Bury:

I, Diva Julio, God of Infinite Space and Time,

I am free, no time for time and invent.

Hold the time.

Paste and join from the Sun and rain.

I'm dumb.

I stopped the clock.

Prevent to advance time.

Keep alive time, space and the rain.

I save time.

Do not sleep ever.

Heart-Sun asked: "Excuse me, Katia, but how do you translate '*detineo*' every time differently?"

"It was exhausting, but then I realized that Caesar was describing every single power that could result in his offspring. In short, the various powers that has you, the Doctor, Tempest and JLH ".

"Interesting," said the Doctor. "You have translated both sides of the paper?"

"In that sense both sides? It is written only from one side".

"Watch it better, and you'll see that both sides are written".

An inscription saying: "*Solum si amended explano, explano cunctus universus*". "Only by deciphering correctly, you will be able to decipher everything". Yes, it seems that the leaf is equipped with a kind of Artificial Intelligence dating back to 2,000 years ago.

The paper reported the following:

Mea fiducia in temporis peregrare est. Mea fiducia impedire est caedem Caesari. Frustra. Hic scriptum Caesari mea manumissio est. Solum si explano emendate, egomet libertus.

Here's the translation:

My decision is to travel through time. My decision is to prevent the death of Caesar. I failed. This document of Caesar is my liberation. Only by deciphering correctly, I'll be free.

"Well, deciphered the entire document," said Heart-Sun. "And now? As we release ours? Here Julius Caesar says freeing himself!"

Gilroy Bury replied: "I don't think Caesar speak of itself. I think that the document has been written by Tempest".

"It is not possible! He, like the hit, was catapulted somewhere", commented Heart-Sun.

The Doctor replied: "Maybe after 2,000 years has changed. In any case, by a laboratory analysis, we found that the Charter is not only original but contains traces of DNA. The document seems to be endowed with Artificial Intelligence. If the author was really Tempest, would be explained".

"Why, though, did not tell us anything?" asked Heart-Sun.

"I think the answer is in the words of the document," said Gilroy Bury. "We must analyze carefully. I hard I understand that words that are repeated each time had a different meaning …"

"… That meant every single power", I finally was able to get myself into the substance of the speech.

The Doctor replied: "You're right JLH. At the beginning it seems talk about Tempest itself, then Heart-Sun, finally you. It seems that my powers are placed here and there in the writing".

I asked: "Yes, however, the document speaks in the first person!"

The Doctor said: "I would surmise that Caesar had all the powers, and that, therefore, they are separated in time. All his descendants have preserved his genetic memory, so that today we did meet everybody".

Ghieroi pose a question rather than logic: "Have you met everyone, because descendants of Caesar. And I what's up?"

I replied: "In my opinion, the document includes you. In fact, you haven't been able to touch and examine. It seems that the message was addressed to you. If we make the case, the second part was a solitary phrase, which seemed to indicate your powers. If you notice at the end, he repeated part of the second term. Maybe there is a message for you".

"Maybe there are. The words used in the last part of the document are particularly strong. The first expression literally would translate: 'My decision is wandering through time'. Tempest wandering must have lost. 'Prevent Caesar's death' could mean: 'Prevent the genetic tree die'. Perhaps, Tempest had discovered something that could cause the extinction of your family. The fact that all Klein are gone would indicate that their lives might be at risk, and maybe even yours! In fact, time travel like? Tempest swaps his DNA with that of a member of his genetic tree. You may have tried to access a member that has no genetic raised children, and therefore has been blocked on his journey, creating a space-time shaking".

"All this, you're deciphering from your document?" severed Heart-Sun.

"No, I'm just assuming the meaning of individual sentences. I think Tempest wanted to leave us a message. I don't know why we have not said anything. Perhaps, as he had forgotten hamlets of his memory, he had forgotten the purpose of the document, which he used to prepare your ancestor of Julius Caesar".

The Doctor added: "And probably tried to protect the paper over time, traveling from generation to generation".

"If you're right," said JLH, "Tempest may need a child to return. Maybe the little Vladimir is not suitable. Maybe some of us should raise a son, to allow Tempest to return. Perhaps that is why you wanted among us, Gilroy Bury: because you become the wife of Heart-Sun, and create a new descendent to Caesar, who has all the powers and may free the Klein".

Chapter XXIII

The darkness did not allow even a little light. If it was a cave, this was not possible to understand, since the four Klein could not reach any wall, any border, while walking in all directions, although it was impossible to orient oneself in that situation. Maybe it was really a black hole.

Suddenly, the place began to shake. The four sought, but one of them did not answer. May be removed too? What happened?

Meanwhile, that JLH suggested to Heart-Sun and Gilroy Bury to marry, the laboratory began to shake. Some object of glass fell to the ground, and broke. A great Thunder exploded in the air, and a man appeared. Members of the Club looked: no one had ever seen, except the Doctor.

"You are Tempest! How is it possible?" Others they looked in their faces, astonished.

"Did you get with the body of your future descendant? You're not arrived as a contemporary Klein".

"Doctor, we have a lot to say. Finally I start to remember everything. When we first met in the future, you've never said he had lost his memory. When did you discover in this mind that I had lost, I told you that I was recovering gradually, but that there was some hidden again".

"Yes, we understand that you wrote the document by deciphering under the guise of Caesar".

"So, you've found it, thankfully. This will free the Klein. But first I have to tell you some important things that concern me".

"We listen carefully you talk".

"When I knew to be capable of time travel, I decided to find out what happened in the past to bring the story perfectly. I noticed that this was impossible, since centuries of incomplete data required the unveiling of historical documents. So, I started with an attempt to discover where the products ended up, so that they might be discovered in the future. At this point, I had to decide which one would be the right time for them to discover. And here I realized that if I had made them discover an era existed before my birth, I could change my future, and I could not ever be born. Finally I decided simply to discover the history, and to put in writing of parallel stories to real ones. Under the assumed name of Ioanan Ceratonia, I began to write children's books. So I wrote the truth, without being shocked story".

"Fascinating, but what happened that you have lost your memory?" asked Heart-Sun.

"Before you travel in time, bought the costumes of the time when I wanted to go. On one occasion, I went into direct contact with Brutus. I was accused of complicity in the murder of his stepfather. I still don't know the genetic link with Caesar. I was arrested. To avoid dying, and more importantly to change history, I went back in time to before being discovered. It was there that included having changed the future. I Became Caesar! From that day I began to travel in time and space, but I began to share my DNA with that of Caesar. Shortly thereafter, I discovered that, actually, I mistook the DNA with the DNA of the new recipient, and I was able to travel exclusively in genetic memory of Caesar ..."

Gilroy Bury interrupted the speech: "From what you're saying, you may not really be a descendant of Caesar, but simply have you been forced by history to become part of his DNA".

The Doctor added: "Tempest! Now I can analyze the true Tempest, I can say that, in fact, your DNA is neither standard nor a non-standard. You have only a fraction of DNA, which is slowly growing!"

"In fact, I won't be able to resist for long. I have to go back into the black hole where I fled when I discovered that my DNA is unstable. Its instability causes my temporal journey, which only Caesar descent through Charlemagne allows me to continue to exist".

"Continue your story, Tempest", said Heart-Sun.

"Where I was finished? ... Yes, when I substituted my DNA with that of Caesar, and then tried to complete my

DNA, to turn Tempest, I discovered that I was now a child, now a grown man, now an old man from the past as a musician and surgery. I was not always in the present, stable, how you can be you, Doctor. When I came back and found out the document, I understand what happened during my first time genetic Exchange: Caesar learned to use the technology of the future, with whom he wrote the document. When I traveled in the 1800's, I discovered that a legend was linked to Caesar. This legend has not been passed if not until 1600, then an ancestor of our enemies is managed through a nightmare to ensure it was cancelled from the memory of mankind ..."

"...Tell us", I said.

"Julius Caesar had known his descendant, a son of Joann and Katia Rajok. This son had inherited all the powers that each Member of the Club. Transmitted power to Caesar, so that it could be used to thwart the rebels led by Brutus. When he returned to his own time, drew up the document, but was unable to use his powers. He was betrayed sooner than expected. So the history is preserved as it was originally done ... now my forces are coming. Now you know what to do. I should be able to free the three Klein. Goodbye".

Disappeared, and a loud roar followed. It appeared the three Klein. Of course, they were full of questions. The

Doctor explained: "You were locked into a space-time vortex. DNA was a joke".

Heart-Sun interjected: "In short, the DNA is a black hole".

Chapter XXIV

Meanwhile, the philosopher, Heart-Sun, entertained with her contention that the DNA would be a black hole, and therefore all Klein had within the DNA of the original Tempest, and here now is the contradiction: how DNA was Tempest? Then, we all have a DNA that contains someone else, and we are in the DNA of anyone else? Finally, we exist or not? In short, while Heart-Sun spoke, a girl listening to just a shiver of sounds from a mouth but her eyes shine. His heart thumped in a completely different way. The head was spinning. Soon I will tell you who it is, and because it was so bad.

Meanwhile, JLH asked: "Are you, or one of you is Tempest?"

Replied Dr. Klein: "Tempest in this present does not exist. So it must use one of us".

J. H. Klein added: "Here I am. I understand that there is no need to intervene in order to bring some order. Our enemies are strong and smart. While we were in the DNA, we understand that there is only one solution".

The Doctor interrupted him: "Really, studying the document of Caesar, also we have found a solution".

Heart-Sun interjected: "Wherefore we have two solutions?"

Tempest said: "We analyzed the situation. From what we know one of my powers can strengthen, Heart-Sun".

"Yes, it's true. But we also know that it is not enough. In addition, our enemies have recovered the power contained in the document", said Heart-Sun.

"That's why we need a new Member in the Universal Club," explained Tempest. "We need a child whose DNA is unknown to our enemies, but always tied with us. We think that if the Doctor could extract DNA from my command that allows me to strengthen, Heart-Sun, this code you can then insert into you. Genetic Scanner serves for this purpose".

The Doctor interjected: "Interesting theory. In any case, it wouldn't be enough, because should then be two known DNA. We need a new body. Because the document does not contain the DNA of Gilroy Bury, is she the solution".

"In that sense I would be the solution?"

"According to the final part of the document you need to have a child by one of us. We have several including you and Heart-Sun is linked in one way or another".

Heart-Sun commented: "In practice we two should get married and have a child? Sister, do you remember that we will have to wait a minimum of nine months for the birth and some years to become adult and mature. Don't you think that the enemies would do everything possible to kidnap him and use it for their own purposes?"

Tempest said: "My memory I came back fully, partly because it mixes with that of my host. In any case, I believe that the purpose of that document was that it arrived in the hands of a child, the son of Heart-Sun and Gilroy Bury. I don't know why, but I feel that it is the only one who can touch that sheet".

Chapter XXV

And so a face was enchanted to hear Heart-Sun speak comically philosophical theory he developed, which would report the DNA with black holes. That face belonged to a girl who was not part of the genetic tree of Heart-Sun, at least so far. In fact, until twenty days ago would never have thought that the marriage would come so quickly. It was organized in secret, so that the four villains were not informed of the fact. So now that I am the 6 o'clock in the morning, we go to rouse Ms. Katia, who in a few hours becomes Mrs.

She didn't want to get up. She hears the door open; he burrowed under the Duvet, and does not want to learn to stand up. The Narrator decided to approach, and poke Katia, who feels compelled to abandon that shelter. It took fifteen minutes of trial. Katia is going to stand up, look at his face, and the narrator says: "If you want that I raise, you must exit. I am a woman. What would think my fiancé if discovered that you are here?" The Narrator was going to quit, but he felt tempted to peep: "Katia, you're not raising! Have you turned? What would your boyfriend if you don't find at his side at City Hall?" Another five minutes, before you finally convinced Katia stand up.

Katia finally came out of the room, and walked towards the kitchen. She opened the fridge, and berates the Narrator feels: "Katia! We have prepared the refreshments in the lounge. Don't eat anything, or you look like a bubble to marriage". "If you don't let me eat, I returned to the bed. This is a threat!" And so it was that he ate three sandwiches, nearly suffocated, with all the Pajamas, and he heard from his mother: "That good! Luckily you're not wearing the wedding dress!" After fifteen minutes, she finally went to his room to fulfill one of the most important gestures that a woman can do in their lives.

6.35. Finally arrived for Katia's time to wear a white dress. For this act he was assisted by his mother and by the seamstress. The Narrator was not permitted to be present, in order to avoid misplaced jealousies. After he was dressed, the Narrator could enter, accompanied by a hairdresser. This woman had a particular haircut: a fringe in front like a pipe, followed by a row in the left area of the head. The hair on the back formed a queue that could envy a Mare, but also a Lion, because wasn't kidding for tonnage. Had a particularly large bag, similar to the one that they use physicians. I wondered: '"isn't that was sent by our enemies to set her up before it can build the solution of our problems?' Circumvented, however, comments about it, and I continued to observe, as a good storyteller. The Hairstylist came to Katya. He opened his bag, on which was written the name of the woman supposedly — Orna Flavia. Took a series of odd tools: glasses mirror with though an odd grayish color (you will then know that it was a cover of lead), combs, brooches, ointments.

Before starting the operation, asked Katia to choose clothes that you would wear in order to choose the most suitable hairstyle. The Decorator began drawing with a comb a line to center of Katia's head from right to left. So could divide your hair in half, tying together the rear ones. Instead, using a labrum formed some braids with hair. When, after the operation, the Narrator looked at Katia, gasped: seemed to have before him a Roman matron! Worthy of a Caesar, walked toward the living room, where he was awaited by his relatives, who, however, had the opportunity to eat. They spent about two hours.

After you have exchanged pleasantries with those present at around 9.00, finally the wedding procession accompanied Katia at City Hall, where he was awaited by Joann and the latter's family, who, if willing, will add its description of the first hours after awakening on arrival at City Hall. I, as a good Knight, I dealt with the bride.

Remember that at the beginning of the previous Chapter Katia was gasping for air? Now it is the turn of Joann. To see his bride, he believed in his eyes: him, descendant of Julius Caesar, the latter's heir, was about to marry a woman like a lady roman accommodated! I finally began to understand why he had become the leader of the Universal Club.

The guests entered the Town Hall. The Mayor awaited them. They were brought into the Hall, celebrating the marriage. Our heroes wore everybody special trinkets developed in the University's Laboratory for detecting bad caps, and to protect themselves.

Having to provide the details of the ceremony, I thought I'd turn around and observe the reactions of the guests. On the other hand, were invited with minimal notice. I In turn their head, I noticed something astonishing, Flavia Orna's hair had formed a kind of wall, which did not allow either to enter or to exit. I dare, and I went up to investigate. When I approached, I said: "Back to follow the marriage. The Doctor instructed me to protect marriage. By the way, you can call me Ornatrix. My hair reaches a length equal to my weight, compared to meter".

I wonder if only I had been left unaware of this new Member of the Club?

Chapter XXVI

It was a beautiful wedding, really. A marriage cannot be perfect if it continues! And then what's a family complete without children? Our couple wasted no time. After a few days of marriage, Katia soon began to grow a belly.

The whole Club was worried: nine months would have been enough? Our neighbors would use their new knowledge against us? Now, we had forgotten that Gilroy Bury is able to adjust the time to its needs. So it was that the nine months for her lasted only nine days! Yes, after only nine days ago was born the small Elisa, Elisa Rajok!

Now there arose another problem: Elisa was a newborn! As would become our Savior? It was decided that each of us would have been a teacher for the dot. Each of us was in charge of to teach a subject. You know that children under three years to assimilate more than larger ones.

The responsibility of JLH was to teach reading and writing. Very difficult undertaking!

J. H. Klein taught mathematics.

The Doctor touched teaches applied Sciences, while Katia's MOM taught her the basics of Science. Joann dad taught her the secrets of Artificial Intelligence.

W. A. Klein delighted with some Music.

Clearly the project to teach the *Omnia sapere* ("Omnia know") was very ambiguous. In fact, if to design Genetic Scanner, our friends had no problem, to design a learning system for a fledgling did not know where to start. At this point was to aid Tempest in person. As you know he can't live out of DNA for long periods. He suggested to MOM Katia to play the little girl with the document by Caesar.

What was the result? After a few minutes he turned that into a foil paper plane that launched. The plane turned back like a boomerang. Already the hidden genius began to see in this future little heroine. He grabbed the sheet immediately as soon as the paper plane went back on its cradle. Katia wanted him to resume, avoiding spoiling him. She turned and lay down prone on top of sheet. Do not let take her up. Meanwhile it continued to "play" with the document, which now gave a particular form: it was identical to the Scanner. It was similar but identical! She had manipulated that ancient paper, which became identical to draft his aunt. Then she pulls her Paper Scanner to Tempest and Katia, the only people present in the room. She pressed the trigger. Then it attacked the paper toward you.

Time because Tempest remains out of DNA, was finished. He couldn't see what happened then. Gilroy Bury found himself suddenly in the University Laboratory, where others were studying ways of training the newcomer. Gilroy Bury said: "Good morning to all. I am Elisa. I needed to talk with you. My mom is at home lying in a baby cot. I removed this sheet that I turned into a Genetic Scanner. Now I'll retrieve DNA from all of you". The Scanner pulls toward his father, her aunt, Klein and JLH. Then he pointed. He vanished from their sight.

He returned in place of little Elisa. Gilroy Bury phoned the workshop immediately, explaining that he had fainted. Her sweet husband replied: "You weren't fainted. You are coming here, but you were Elisa. It seems that has already started his job!"

Heart-Sun suddenly told the crowd: "We have to defeat our enemies. Thanks to this document, I share my DNA with each of you. In this way I will be able to use your strongest points under any circumstances". Then he said: "Excuse me, but I must have fainted".

"No," said his sister. "Elisa communicated with us through you".

Heart-Sun said: "Great!"

"I wouldn't say," commented the Doctor. "To communicate, it needs to exchange his DNA with one of ours. To do so one of us is unable to be present. Also I am concerned about his strategy. Jeopardize any of us".

Heart-Sun said: "About the presence, simply bring it here …"

The Doctor replied: "No. long as it's not newborn will allow us to understand what it says".

In any case, the day after Heart-Sun and Gilroy Bury led the little Elisa. The Doctor said: "We have to find out what is the power of it, before it becomes dangerous to him and others".

Tempest, as Klein's grandfather said: "When I exchange my DNA over time, I return the DNA to the rightful owner. Elisa instead swaps her body with that of another person, and without necessarily genetically related".

The Doctor added: "No, it is not a simple exchange of bodies. Otherwise it would be impossible, or metempsychosis for you and for me. No, I think instead of 'Park' someone within the DNA as do you, uses his body as 'par-parking', but only for the fraction of DNA that does not serve its purpose".

Heart-Sun looked white: "What did you say? Call a municipal policeman directing the traffic of DNA? I did not understand anything of what you said!"

"I try to be clearer. However, during the gestation period, those that dot are initially the fetus begins to form a genetic code that would provide a lot of information which will be born: the amount of hands, feet, fingers, limbs, hair color, eyes, etc. Also provides other information pertaining to the personal tastes of the person who is to be born. Not for nothing each fetus reacts to certain stimuli that can be hunger, thirst, but also the sounds from music, from someone's voice, the sound of some object, and so on. We who have nonstandard DNA we have in our genetic code of more data. And here we come to what is Elisa: transfers its DNA in our bodies, which duplicates and temporarily copies the DNA in his body. It restrains the fraction of DNA that you need. So if you use your body, you will retain the immense force that you, together with your liquid gluing and your infusion jar. If it will use your wife, it held that information which will become fast folding time".

"We have created a monster?"

"That's why I want to understand in detail that heroic ability has. If we use to solve our contention, could kill the host body, and perhaps her. She must be trained".

The Doctor changed his expression, and began to talk by saying: "The Doctor is right on what they are capable of. Unfortunately I do not know what would happen if they were to put the host body, but preserve DNA copy in me. Yes, I am a human backup. My plan is as follows: we will use your skills to defeat enemies. Now I'm leaving them assimilate into my body. I'll tell you when I am ready to act using my body. By the way, call me Miss Backup".

The Doctor now said: "I talked through me, right? It seemed to pass out".

"Yes," replied Heart-Sun. "And said he is assimilating our powers to act alone".

"Hum. Therefore it seems that is doing a copy of save our DNA".

"Yes, indeed, said he chose a heroic name: Miss Backup".

Chapter XXVII

Noor al-'Iskenderun (نوردنكسإلا) is a famous oilman Southeastern Anatolia. He owns the oldest oil refinery of Turkey.

Reportedly he was a descendant of Alexander the Great. In fact, it is said that his ancestor was born at Issus in 333 BC. Hatay al-'Iskenderun, in the 9th century AD became Muslim. In the mid-twentieth century, the family al-'Iskenderun moved from Iskenderun, where he had resided for centuries, in easternmost Turkey. It was said that in the Southeastern Anatolia had been discovered a new liquid substance, black. In 1955 the family al-'Iskenderun founded the first Batman's oil company.

Noor was born in 1971. Now the al-'Iskenderun refinery had become one of the largest in the world. In 1990 he entered the University, because he was intrigued: oil has a DNA? If yes, could be exploited? When, in 1997, he graduated, still had not answered his question. However, he returned to his homeland, because his father, Abdullah al-'Iskenderun, now more than eighty, was dying. When he arrived at Batman, Abdullah announced that he had been chosen to head the family business. Also handed him the parchment, centuries old, they were given some information on the origin of his family.

The document reveals that in 1034 his ancestor was born, Hassan-I Sabbah, who in 1094, now sixty, took as a concubine a descendant of Hatay al-'Iskenderun, from where they had a son, who was generously allowed to inherit surname from his mother.

The document describes the fortress of Hassan-I Sabbah as a paradise, rich in a beautiful garden, with beautiful girls, four fountains from which sprang the wine, milk, honey and water, in the likeness of the rivers of paradise. According to the document, was under the influence of a drug, now known as hashish (from *al-Hashīshiyyūn*, the name of the sect founded by Hassan-I Sabbah), who was conceived the young Hulagu al-'Iskenderun.

In addition, the document contained a map, an itinerary to reach the seat of assassins to Masyaf (مصياف). Here in the 12th century lived and ruled Jebel al-'Iskenderun. Upon his death, his sons were in the city of Iskenderun and resided there until about 1950.

There was also an architectural map of the fortress. After the death of his father, Noor made contact with the Rector of the University where he graduated, to create a partnership and to perform genetic experiments on oil. He was flanked by several students that the University periodically sent to Batman. Many of these students, upon contact with the oil in the laboratory, began to develop new physical abilities. According to the Doctor, Noor mingled hashish oil. It was not determined whether someone else besides Noor has drunk this deadly cocktail. From what we have been able to determine so far, Noor became faster and stronger, and he also developed a super-hearing.

As a direct descendant of Hassan-I Sabbah and Jebel al-'Iskenderun seems to have decided to continue to govern. The recent coup attributed by the UN to Sheikh al-Jebel we believe was organized by Noor al-'Iskenderun. For nearly a year we're investigating to find out who is Sheikh al-Jebel. There are no photographs, fingerprints and such. Now that Universal Club has a new Member, Miss Backup, we hope to strengthen investigations, although Gilroy Bury has not yet fully returned in force. In fact, his Super-speed and its ability to flex time don't always work properly.

Also, throughout this period, we no longer knew anything about Genna'ro the Brand, Rector, Incubus and Poliglottix. We hope that you join this terrorist, Sheikh al-Jebel. Soon we will organize an expedition to Masyaf.

Chapter XXVIII

I know I should be concerned about the situation in Turkey, but lately I can't think of anything else. Recently I returned back in time to change the future. I never imagined that I would have totally changed my future. I have a brother, from which I could never have children. In the Universal Club joined members that weren't there before my departure. None of us knew a document written by Caesar thanks to Tempest. So we changed the whole future of the world, but also ours.

At least now I know why my kids were born with genetic abnormalities that I couldn't explain. The "influence *bis*" ("*Encore*)" that we were supposed to fight back in time, making sure that you don't develop, in fact, does not exist. I am increasingly certain: this disease was caused by genetic abnormalities of my children, are derived from the marriage between me and Heart-Sun. Thankfully now I know that we are brothers, twins, and therefore we have avoided this disaster that would put the whole world to its knees.

Unfortunately, something has changed. If before leaving some Club members were good, now are our worst enemies. It seems that their new base is Turkey. Only today I understand that we had been manipulated from the beginning to create a biological weapon. We knew that someone had betrayed us, but not to the point of letting us marry and have children with a dangerous virus.

I don't know what will happen to the future of our planet. We could go back and edit again the future. But what else would happen? We could lead to something worse! We could become us bad! No, the time has come to tackle the foe.

How do we manage? They have trained dozens of people, changing its DNA. We could try to convince some of them to join us. We could turn to any Government to create a super army. Now that my brother is a leader, will surely like you recommend. Not forgetting my sweet granddaughter, this is very powerful, although only just. According to Tempest, she is the key that will allow us to win the battle. However, I still haven't figured out how to succeed. The only idea I have is that you get all the DNA enemies, but we don't know how many they are.

Nevertheless, we still have no evidence that Genna'ro the Brand, the Rector, Incubus and Poliglottix have joined Sheikh al-Jebel, which also does not yet know the identity. Has a non-standard DNA? Is able to fight against us? Might be an enemy to us both for them? Might change, becomes a good person? We hope you find the answers to these questions.

To return to the initial discourse, there is really something that I care about, more than many others. If before time travel I had a husband, now that I'm back to the present, I'm alone. Never will I find the right man for me?

Hey! That's going on over there? Let me open the door. I was in an empty classroom at correcting the tests of the last examination. I had to stop in my thoughts rambled. I just opened the door: how many people! Hey! There is a man, his right leg is bent, from the knee to the foot is on the ground. The other leg struggled to keep it standing. Meanwhile he tries to lean on the wall; from the left shoulder is pouring blood. Is hurt! Cry: "Bring him in the infirmary! There we have everything you need to cure it".

Two attendants of University assist the stranger. I am with them. I help to bind the wound. "What's it called?" I ask the man that we are treating. "What happened?"

"My name is Noor", I respond with a breath. "Someone shot me. I came to visit my old University".

"Why they fired?"

"I don't know. I was getting into when I heard a loud roar, and then I found myself in this State".

"We have to find out just who he was".

"She's thoughtful, doctor".

"Thank You. However, I am a Professor of this University".

"Then surely knows Mrs. Ivanovo. I heard it is the best teacher of genetics. It is a pity that when I studied here she isn't there".

"You know what? It's really lucky. I am Professor Mary Ivanovo".

"It's really you in person?"

"Yes, in person".

"It's a real shame that I have already graduated. At that time there was a genetic teacher like her. Probably would have been more enjoyable study. She bears no resemblance at all to that prehistoric teacher". Then he coughed. From his mouth spat blood.

"Are having too many emotions. You'd better calm yourself, dear Noor. Now I leave here to rest. I'll be back later to see how he is. Meanwhile do I put someone outside the door, you never know what might happen. The police certainly will do an inspection of the perimeter of the block. Goodbye, Noor". I wanted to keep talking with him. It looks so youthful. I never said that you had graduated when still there was one professor. He must be older than me, though it seems my same age, if not younger.

"I'm sorry Mary, can I ask you something?"

"Tell me as well, John. ... How long have I called you so! Will be at least five years that I had gotten accustomed to appeal JLH! Anyway, tell me as well".

"I like this TWENTY-EIGHTH Chapter you're writing. Why not make a research to find out who was this Noor?"

"I don't know his last name. And then, it might be a nickname".

"You don't remember that many nicknames were born right here, at the University?"

I checked in the annals of the University. I found only one Noor, "Noor al-'Iskenderun" but had graduated in the 1990s. This was young, Noor but not enough. It's probably just a nickname.

In two hours, I finished correcting tests. With all the compliments that I received, I decided to give a higher rating to all my students. So, after I got rid of my school work, I went to see how he was Noor.

As I opened the door, a cheerful voice I said: "Here's my favorite teacher! The only one I can interrogate, but can't give me a bad rating".

"This is to be seen. Now, I will visit. If you notice that something is wrong, will receive a bad vote ... heath".

"I will do as he commands, doctor! However, we can speak with a familiar language?"

"OK," I replied sobbing, and took my left hand over her breasts under her chin. "The injury doesn't seem to be serious. You will be able to return very soon to move the arm and walking. A good night's sleep will be refreshing".

"Yes, but I won't have to not spend the night at the University?"

"You have accommodation?"

"Really, I didn't. I came straight from the airport to the University. I had to share this evening".

"It is a *toccata and fugit,* eh?"

"Yes, I have come here on business. So I wanted to take the opportunity to come and visit my old University. Can you suggest a place to stay?" In ask me this question, struck his left eye, as if to tell me 'Why didn't you guests tonight?'

"I think my brother will have no objections to providing a bed".

"He lives far away?"

"No, since she is married, moved into my own apartment building". He looked at me smiling. It seems happy to spend the night in the apartment next to mine.

I Called Joann. I asked him if he could host it. I replied: "Absolutely, no! I don't want a stranger in my house!"

"Now, I cannot host it myself!"

"Why don't you send in a hotel?"

"Need help!"

"My house is not a hospital. Call an ambulance, and let us bring!"

"So you'd be the leader of the most important emergency team in the world? You're not even hospitable".

"OK. Now I feel my wife that my sister has saddled his host, to my house!"

Despite this note of sarcasm, I'm sure in his heart was glad to host it.

19.00 o'clock my brother and our new friend we did lead to housing. "That cosy home!" exclaimed upon entering.

"Yes, all say so," muttered my brother with clenched fist in front of the mouth.

"Yes, did it say?" asked Noor.

"No, I said, thanks for the compliment". Heart-Sun was blushing. Bearing in mind that, normally, who makes him blush roasts, the situation could only escape it by hand.

We settled into the living room, where there was also the little Elisa in his pit. My granddaughter was playing with the butterflies that ran above the box, playing Beethoven's *Für Elise* notes. It did not seem intrigued by the guest. My sister-in-law, meanwhile, brought us something to drink. I offered to help her, but he refused. A moment before Joann had gone into the kitchen to talk to her, probably to explain the situation, namely the fact of having to accommodate Noor. When Katya arrived with the tray smiled to all of us, then went back into the kitchen to begin cooking for four. Her husband, however, came up with a nice idea.

"Tell me, Noor, she knows pizza?" he asks.

"Thirty years will not eat one". Having said that, we laughed, thinking about the fact that maybe 30 years ago wasn't even born!

So I went from my sister-in-law to announce that he would order the pizza. Joann ordered his usual *Diavola*, Katia instead demanded a *Pizza Margherita* baby, not burdening her milk; I ordered a pizza with seafood (*Frutti di Mare*), while Noor called for a *Vegetarian*. Then he said, joking: "For those who like me are a vegetarian, pizza is a real treat!"

The pizza seemed more happy than usual, yet it was the same as where we order pizza ever. Perhaps the presence of Noor has made it better? I think the pizza is the most important invention in the history of mankind. Should I analyze my DNA Scanner, to find out if you have some property to be added to my powers?

Or how it is done later! It is better that I go to my apartment. Hi all. Goodnight everyone, even you, my darling, Elisa.

I go out from my brother's House and I go to the apartment. As I lay in bed, I miss. When I rise from bed, the nightstand, where is placed the lamp. There is a sheet where I read: *"Tracking Little Course. The Club needs a Seventh member. My parents cannot move"* ('Tracking Little Horn. The Club needs a Seventh member. My parents cannot move'). Elisa Rajok, you want to tell me? Are you a Little Horn? I am tired; I did not want to understand the meaning leaving by Elisa.

Chapter XXIX

Finally I sleep, and what happens? Elisa starts to cry. She has never cried as tonight! Indeed, the night never cries. It is always quiet. Yet during the dinner didn't seem bothered by the guest. I can't take sleeping. I'm desperate. I should get up early, go to University, take a Science lesson, gather with the Club and spend time with Noor. If you don't sleep, though, how can I focus in the face of all these commitments?

I have an idea. I get up, and within in the apartment opposite. I could get into it with my ability to move in space, but I wouldn't be seen by Noor. Luckily, I have a copy of this key. I enter without making noise. I approach my nephew's room. I seemed to hear a strange noise coming from the room. Perhaps it is my hearing wild-eyed I betrays. When a person is tired, my ears don't work properly. I take in Elisa, arm which quiets down for a moment, and then start squealing. Strangely my relatives were left to sleep.

A hand touches his shoulder to me suddenly. What a scare! I turn trembling, and I see Noor. "Sorry if I scared," she tells me with subheading. "I was trying to sleep, because he couldn't get to sleep. I don't have to like a lot".

Meanwhile, Joann and Katia arrive. "What's wrong? Because disturbed Elisa?" asks my brother.

"Really, she was crying so hard, don't allow me to sleep".

"We had heard crying, but we couldn't move from bed. The pizza was really heavy", said Katia, leaving me a little dumbfounded. A portion of the paper was clarified. Why, though, Elisa has them blocked? Maybe he meant me? Could not directly exchange of DNA?

"Listen," I say, "why don't you let me take your daughter with me? Maybe it will fall asleep. Maybe it's a bit restless for the presence of Noor, who does not know".

Katia turned to Elisa: "You mustn't be afraid of Noor. Is a friend of ours". Then agreed that bring in my apartment.

I took her to bed with me, I hold in my arms, and I can finally fall asleep. Hey, what's up? It is already the dawn? Or am I dreaming? This place is familiar to me. There have already been a few years ago. Here I was coming to change the future and to save the world for the first time. Hey but Elisa is here with me, that he sleeps quiet. What happened? Where we've brought Elisa? This however is not the same place of the Grand Canyon where we at the time. You could leave me a clue, Elisa? Or maybe it's on that sheet? Behold, the pajama has no pockets. Where I will have left the paper? What was written? For a moment, but I am no longer in pajamas. I have pants that I arrive just below the knees. I am wearing a blue blouse.

I have a straw hat on his head, and Brown boots. I'm dressed as an Explorer, and without my usual green.

Let me look around. I see a hut. A man sits near a fire. Certainly, he isn't the temperature warms up. I approach and try to talk to him: "Hey, good man. Can I talk to her?"

"Tell me? That tells me there is no one else on this side of the Grand Canyon. Tell me Lady".

"Who is it?"

"I am a Navajo. My name is *Inde Diné*. How Come you are here all alone?"

"I could ask the same question to you too".

"I was born in Texas. Due to some changes in my life I decided to move here, solo new harmonization with Mother Earth. Now he wants to give me an answer? Why is it here?"

"I'm looking for one person".

"Unfortunately I do not know anyone here".

Too bad, I was hoping that would help me track down the seventh member of the Club. At least, reasoning a bit I, i.e. the Doctor, Heart-Sun, Tempest, Gilroy Bury, Ornatrix and JLH we 6. It seems that my niece wanted a seventh member to win the battle. If you brought me here, must have had a reason. I try to put another question to this gentleman.

"Listen to a curiosity. By chance his surname means 'Little Horn'?"

"No, my name, 'Inde', is the name of the Apache people, from which are descended the Navajo. My surname, 'Diné', meaning 'The people', and remember that I belong to the Navajo, meaning "cultivated field in a Little Course of water' (or "fields adjoining a ravine")".

It is interesting. Let me double check the paper. Yes, I misread. I tired eyes. There was written: *Tracking Little Course. The Club needs a Seventh member. My parents cannot move* ('Tracking Little Course. The Club needs a Seventh member. My parents cannot move'). Yes, Elisa was asking me to trace a Navajo. Probably wants to be among us Diné Inde.

What happened? I'm in bed. The alarm indicates that the time of getting up to go to College. Can I have dreamed? Elisa is here in bed with me. I am at my house; on the other side of the world I dreamed or visited last night.

While the small carryover Elisa at home by his mother, crossing Noor, who tells me: "I'm so sorry. I have to share. A problem arose. I have to return to Turkey. Please consult the appointment the next time". How sad! My "man" if he goes, and he doesn't know what I feel for him. Maybe one day he will read from my diary (not going to happen, if you won't be admitted into the Club, because this diary can be read only by members of the Club and by passionate readers like you, good people who care about the welfare of humanity).

Chapter XXX

The time has come because the Club together. Yesterday we received a very special visit. Home of Heart-Sun was found an invitation to attend a convention, organized by a certain Dan Menise Sky. I, as a "journalist" of the group have been chosen with Heart-Sun and the Doctor to participate.

Arrived on the place, in Reykjavik, we set off towards the *National Gallery Listasafn*, which is often used for exhibitions in themes. In fact, on this occasion, there was a particular theme, "The Ice, the Glaciers & the Icebergs". We found a rich exhibition of photographs, paintings (probably not originals), scale models that depicted glaciers and icebergs around the world. After a few minutes of our arrival, we were encouraged to settle down in our seats, because Dan Menise Sky would have pronounced the speech in which he explained his latest discovery. Hypothetically, we supposed that he had to be a researcher, perhaps specializing in ice. Below is the transcript of the most important parts of his speech.

"I'm happy to see you all gathered here along with me. The few who know me call me a hermit because I spent many years of my life studying the glaciers directly on field. As you know, my research allowed me to make an exceptional discovery. Before I tell you about it, though, let me tell you a little story of glaciers. At the very least, a theory that prompted me to do research on ice.

"According to historians, the glaciers have existed for thousands of years. Not only that, but they claim that over time the density of glaciers has decreased. This theory, however, contradicts another, namely the fact that, at one time, the Earth was a planet covered in lava. How to reconcile these two theories? Since no one is arguing the latter, by way of evidence, I wanted to take issue with the first theory. And so I went to study the glaciers on the highest mountains in the world, but also the mountains of ice called iceberg. Studying the latter, in fact, I understand that the glaciers were formed very recently. Not only that, but they are one of the main reasons for which the man dies after only 70-80 years of life expectancy.

"Yes, at one time, there were no glaciers, and the man used to live longer! The famous Methu'shael is said to have lived 969 years beauty! How Come today man lives so cheap? Remember what happened nearly 4,500 years ago? The man began to misbehave. After 120 years, in 2370 BC fell to the waters of the Global Deluge. Already, 'fell', submerging the planet. Only eight men and some animals, refugees in the Ark built by Divine Providence, were saved. After that, mankind departed from scratch. But also the Planet sailed with a number of structural changes.

"With the Deluge great changes came, for example, the life span of humans dropped very rapidly. Prior to the Flood the waters above the expanse shielded out some of the harmful radiation and that, with the waters gone, cosmic radiation genetically harmful to man increased. Incidentally, any change in radiation would have altered the rate of formation of radioactive carbon-14 to such an extent as to invalidate all radiocarbon dates prior to the Flood.

"With the sudden opening of the 'springs of the watery deep' and 'the floodgates of the heavens,' untold billions of tons of water deluged the Planet. This may have caused tremendous changes in Planet's surface. The Planet's crust is relatively thin (estimated at between 30 km [20 mi] and 160 km [100 mi] thick), stretched over a rather plastic mass thousands of kilometers in diameter. Hence, under the added weight of the water, there was likely a great shifting in the crust. In time new mountains evidently were thrust upward, old mountains rose to new heights, shallow sea basins were deepened, and new shorelines were established, with the result that now about 70 percent of the surface is covered with water. This shifting in the Planet's crust may account for many geologic phenomena, such as the raising of old coastlines to new heights. It has been estimated by some that water pressures alone were equal to '2 tons per square inch,' sufficient to fossilize fauna and flora quickly.

— See *The Biblical Flood and the Ice Epoch,* by D. Patten, 1966, p. 62.

"Where is all that water now? Evidently it is right here on the Planet. It is believed that there was a time when the oceans were smaller and the continents were larger than they are now, as is evidenced by river channels extending far out under the oceans. It should also be noted that scientists have stated that mountains in the past were much lower than at present, and some mountains have even been pushed up from under the seas. As to the present situation, it is said that 'there is ten times, as much water by volume in the ocean as there is land above sea level. Dump all this land evenly into the sea, and water would cover the entire Planet, one and one-half miles deep.' — *National Geographic,* January 1945, p. 105.

"Yes, the man after the Deluge went from an average of over 800 years, less than 200 and, within a few centuries, at an average under 100 years. At least 3,500 years, few humans have exceeded the century of life. Probably from sixty to one hundred generations were born during this period. If the man had continued to live with her previous media generations would be only three or four.

"And so we arrive at my discovery. I found a way to transfer and glaciers cover the layers of atmosphere ruined by pollution. Thanks to a researcher that soon I will present you, will ensure the next human generation, if not at that moment, to live at least 1,000 years! Are you happy?" A pelting of hands followed. Of course, even a buzz caused by disbelief.

Meanwhile, we saw a person get on the podium that we already knew. Dan Menise Sky began to speak, saying: "I present my huge contributor, Noor al-'Iskenderun, the only contact I've had in my research. He has developed a machine to transfer the icy waters of our Planet in the sky. We"ll have more land, we will live ten times longer, and all this thanks to the enterprise of Noor al-'Iskenderun".

No thought in our eyes. Noor was the same student who years ago studying at our universities, and is not even slightly aged. Could be he the terrorist collaborator with Sheikh al-Jebel Turkish coup? We have to investigate.

Just got back to HQ, we mentioned the fact. The Doctor took Noor's defenses: "You said you had the same first and last name. But you know very well that age does not match! Maybe Sheikh al-Jebel has used the identity of Noor al-'Iskenderun in the coup, making us believes that they are two separate people".

At this point it was de rigueur to Masyaf expedition. Unfortunately, not all of us were in force. In addition, what we could do with small Elisa? However powerful, was also helpless. While we were discussing what to do,

Elisa's mother intervened: "before we return everyone Masyaf together on the Grand Canyon".

Chapter XXXI

At this point the log I feel obliged, but have also been authorized by the other, to report that Heart-Sun has designed a very special means of transport. It is a hovercraft capable of moving even under the sea and, thanks to special wings, to fly. Thanks to a link with the Scanner, in addition, we have entered a biometric security system really only: the hovercraft can only be used by members of the Universal Club. Not only that, but even the medium behaves differently according to the one from which it will be guided, and sundry by its healthy state. We named it "Heart-Craft".

Since we have little time to track and recruit Inde Diné, Gilroy Bury guides the hovercraft so you can take us quickly to the Grand Canyon. We decided that I will remain in the Heart-Craft in expectation and with Miss Backup, while the Doctor, Heart-Sun, Gilroy Bury and Tempest from Inde Diné.

This is probably the easiest mission since the beginning of our adventures.

That strange sounds coming from the speakers of central command of the hovercraft: Crash! Crash! And still crashes! "Ready! What's up? You hear me?" Nothing, I hear the same noise, but they do not respond.

"We are under attack! Sheikh al-Jebel is here! It seems that he has come for Inde Diné", told me on the radio Gilroy Bury.

Move the narrative close to the home of Inde Diné. In fact, the Heart-Craft was left at the port of San Diego. Our heroes have moved due to the ability of the Doctor and Tempest to be conveyed spatially.

Near the home of Inde Diné found Sheikh al-Jebel ready to capture Inde Diné. Sheikh al-Jebel appeared as a middle-aged man. Beside him there was our knowledge, Dan Menise Sky and their acolytes. "Who are you doing here? With Little Course we almost finished our harvest; but, because the latter two are newly arrived, today we will complete".

Dan Menise Sky ice he sprayed against Heart-Sun, who smoothly answered: "Who do you think you are? Don't you know that ice makes me stronger?" And so he sprays her liquid gluing. However, the other replied: "How stupid you are! Resend me what I control smoothly. By the way, call me Glacier!"

Since nobody was bothering Little Course, Heart-Sun led to his wife: "Go, and bring it with your powers to Heart-Craft". Although he had not yet fully recovered, he managed to carry it fast enough in San Diego.

While Heart-Sun and Glacier fought among themselves, Tempest was trying to defend himself from ten Simian that had thrown upon him. Instead the Doctor began a fight against Sheikh al-Jebel, trying to discover the true relationship between him and Noor. Using the Scanner, she tried to send them a virus. He fell to the ground. After a while, his skin began to change. He became the youngest. He was Noor! The Doctor was appalled and motionless. Noor took the opportunity to give checkmate.

Heart-Sun breaks free from Glacier and went to the aid of her sister, leaving inter alia the possibility of joining forces with Tempest, who cried out: "Come and help me! I need your help!" While approached the Doctor, Noor struck him, sending him to KO. While he tried to get up, he threw even more Glacier Ice and was immobilized. Tempest was left alone. Although he was able to move through space, it was impossible to defend against. Glacier joined his forces with those of Noor, and managed to defeat even Tempest.

"Hey! That happened?" I ask Gilroy Bury. "Where are the others?"

"It looks like we weren't the only ones interested in Inde Diné. By the way, meet Inde Diné".

I try to communicate with others, but to no avail. We decide to stay in the Heart-Craft, which is definitely the safest place. Finally, after three hours of waiting, I can hear a voice.

Heart-Sun had remained unconscious for three hours. After he woke up, he began to look around. And he said, stammering: "That ... What have you done? ... I have you forsaken me?" Then he tried to contact the Heart-Craft. On the other hand, responded: "We're JLH well. And there, how are you? Gilroy Bury led rescued Little Course".

"I am alone. My sister and Tempest are back at Heart-Craft?"

"Why Is That? I'm not with you?" Then JLH attempted to communicate with their radio.

"Pretty darn thing this radio. I like how it was designed. By the way, I kept for you to know that you cannot communicate with your friends. Goodbye by Sheikh al-Jebel".

JLH immediately communicated the fact to Heart-Sun: "Were abducted. Who knows what atrocities would let them!"

We had to become seven. And now we are not diminished, nor do we know what role will have Little Course. Meanwhile, I do share the Heart-Craft. I depart to the North Pacific Ocean and then take a flight to reach Heart-Sun in order to return home.

Chapter XXXII

Back at home, we are all impatient to interrogate Little Course, to find out what's special about. Unfortunately we have no Tempest, nor the ability of the Doctor, nor can we use Genetic Scanner, which was seized along with her. Moreover it seems that Elisa will not communicate. Perhaps she no longer knows which way to turn.

Little Course tells us about some history. Nothing indicates that he was of particular genetic powers. But Elisa wanted it to be one of ours. Not only that, but even the enemies wants, and is likely to return alive. We will succeed the next time to defend ourselves from their attack?

The day is about to end, when I remember that somewhere we had preserved the old Genetic Scanner. Gilroy Bury goes the University archive and returns with the first Scanner! Help, how does it work? Thank goodness that brought with it the second, although we don't know how it works, but at least it is connectable to your PC!

After a few attempts, Heart-Sun manages to connect not only with PC but also with Little Course. Result? His DNA is nonstandard, but can't figure out which exploits can accomplish.

For now it is good to know that eventually we will be able to count on its full potential.

Finally, we return to our homes. Little Course goes home from the Doctor, being absent for more forces.

In the evening, I decide to watch TV. On the news I hear a series of important announcements.

A group of researchers has discovered where located Noah's Ark is! The Turkish Government has granted to a Turkish researcher, Noor al-'Iskenderun, to organize an expedition to recover it.

Dan Menise Sky announces that soon his findings will be made available for the benefit of humanity.

Dr. Livings isolated DNA of Julius Caesar. It will be attempted cloning!

That's weird; it seems that our enemies have managed to penetrate into the ether! Their intentions always seem clearer. I decide to call others to extraordinary reasons. Also, I invite you to join us as well, so that it can again Ornatrix help.

Before describing the extraordinary meeting, we remember those who are our enemies.

On the one hand, we must fight against:

- Genna'ro The Brand, able to stop time of bodies;

- Incubus (Rector), able to sleep his opponents;

- Legend (David Livingstone, Dr. Livings), able to read people's genetic history.

Remember that for each of them we have already developed the necessary defenses.

- Poliglottix (Moradh Lifneh), capable of speaking any language.

On the other hand, we have:

- Sheikh al-Jebel (Noor al-Iskenderun), an oilman who remains forever young thanks to its regenerative power. He managed to hide his powers to the Doctor! Can combine her powers with those of others. Who knows what other powers will have;

- Glacier (Dan Menise Sky), able to change the texture of the ice.

My fear is that the first four will join the other two. Remember that they have a number of acolytes.

What follows, it will be a very long night. We are all at home of Heart-Sun. We didn't want to wake the little Elisa. On the other hand, were already all there; only I was missing.

Heart-Sun, being in charge of the University Club, took the floor:

"Thanks to the reporting of JLH, all we were able to follow the news this evening. We need to understand what the precise intentions of our enemies are. For example, why have kidnapped my sister and Tempest? What will Noah's ark? How will 'benefit' humanity? Cloning Julius Caesar Going what will happen?" We analysed each point, leading to various hypotheses.

Noor is just in love with the Doctor? Or maybe you want to take advantage of it, making the brainwashing?

If Noah's ark is damaged, they will oblige Tempest to travel through time? In that way be able to prevent him from using the powers he has? Who want to take advantage of its ability to create storms to recreate a new Flood?

Therefore, the purpose of the ark will save the wicked, and destroy humanity?

Humanity has the ability to improve their lives, reaching one thousand years. If he is swept away by a flood, who 'benefit'?

Why Legend wants to clone Julius Caesar? He and his want to conquer the world under the rule of a new Roman Empire? Looking online we found the *Secta Juliorum Caesaris*.

Suddenly Gilroy Bury stands up and starts talking: "You must forgive me if I remained silent since aunt Mary and Tempest were abducted; but I tried all day to contact them. Sheikh al-Jebel, when it came in the guise of a young Noor, had already figured out how to help tell you what danger we were. At the same time, I was able to connect with him, discovering the existence of Little Course. Again, I struggled to connect with ours. Recently, though, I was able to contact Tempest. I made a backup of your current DNA. It has been modified. All our enemies have deployed together. Using the modified camera are isolating the DNA of Julius Caesar, so that Tempest is transformed. It is likely that he will lead the expedition to retrieve the Ark of Noah, in which to put animals will feel save and only people with modified DNA already selected. Then using the powers of Glacier and petroleum installations will melt the ice around the world. After that humanity is dead, they will evaporate the excess water, to add a new atmosphere to the Planet. This will allow you to live ten times more, but humanity will start from scratch, and this time with only the aunt that hero good!"

"Little Elisa, thanks for your surveys!" said dad Joann. "The world is in the hands of madmen!"

If the challenge had to be easier to retrieve Little Course, what follows is the hardest ever addressed.

Chapter XXXIII

We decided to join us too. I just couldn't get on the mountains of Ararat on the same side for which climbed them. Ornatrix puts at your disposal its long hair. It created a sort of ladder that allowed us to get on the other side of the mountain. With some hair, it also formed a protective wall.

When we climbed, we met the big enemy team. Tempest had become Julius Caesar, and was commanding them. The Doctor was unable to move.

Julius Tempest Caesar used his abilities to capture Little Course.

Some of their acolyte's oil flooded there. Yes, they fused themselves oil and hashish. Ornatrix formed a "Parasol" (or "umbrella"). Heart-Sun was struck by boiling oil. Being a source of heat, he strengthened immediately, and it launched against those guys like a bowling ball. And so did strike!

Suddenly Miss Backup began to cry. Legend and Incubus had made sleep so that they could intervene. Then they caused a nightmare that almost made me crazy. Genna'ro The Brand stopped his movements.

With Miss Backup K.O. the situation began to worsen. Trying to break free, continued to exchange genetic information into a kind of local network gone wild. It was used as a server for sending genetic virus to all of us. Cybernetic waves we were doing literally drive you crazy. As Tempest, she too was finished under the control of the crazies!

Step the narrative a Little Course.

I observe Heart-Sun that, after the strike, he finds himself blocked by the virus sent to him. Observe others, and I realize that, for some reason, the virus is not working against me. Tempest, controlled by DNA of Julius Caesar, I had captured. Maybe he has genetically isolated from viral attacks Miss Backup. I think I want to immerse myself in this soup of oil and hashish to use me against the Universal Club.

"Now you'll see your ex-friends die. You will use your power to save some people who show you, in order to ensure that mankind continue to multiply, even if more slowly".

"Of that power are you talking about?"

"Yet you have not understood? The Doctor has kept you clueless?"

"The Doctor I broke down, and didn't find anything in me".

"It's always like that. It pretends not to know anything, but you know more than necessary. It knows every little letter of your DNA. You could read no more than you".

"Fortunately also Sheikh al-Jebel has managed to discover your skills in time".

"What are you talking about? I am not able to do anything special. I have captured flawlessly".

"You can do a lot. This virus comes from your blood".

"This is not possible!"

"We were able to visit the breweries that Gilroy Bury you led. When you took away the blood, she did not know that we had installed software on your computer. So we recovered your genetic data, and with them we were able to create the virus that will destroy them".

"Please save them!"

"Maybe we can save them. As long as you do something for me before it's too late".

"Tell Me".

"You have to touch some people who I will appoint unto you. You'll help resist the climatic changes that take place after the melting glaciers. They will have to get used to live near the tar. Unfortunately, not all selected belong to the Group of standard DNA, but we need to ensure the multiplication of mankind".

"Why would you destroy humanity?"

"The man has exceeded all limits in its atrocities. Only a select few can afford to stay. The Flood never taught you anything?"

"You're not a Judge Almighty!"

"I have commanded the world over two thousand years ago. And I will continue to do so for another thousand years!"

"You're crazy! Gives you time your brain! Your project should not be completed".

"You'll see dying friend and even your people. Do what I command you, and you will save anyone".

"I want all you save!"

"Do You See? You already begin to accept that the new Flood can happen!"

"You don't know a thing. In the aftermath of the flood, God decreed: 'Never again shall I call down evil upon the ground on man's account, because the inclination of the heart of man is bad from his youth up; and never again shall I deal every living thing a blow just as I have done. For all the days the earth continues, seed sowing and harvest, and cold and heat, and summer and winter, and day and night, will never cease'. Since you want to delete the glaciers, not the Planet, you can't do this thing!" – Genesis 8:21, 22.

"Shut Up! 'The imagination of man's heart is evil', and deserves to be deleted".

"You're not the Judge on the Planet! It is your right to do so!"

"Now the process is started. It may not come back. With these stupid requests you're lost much time. Probably won't be able to treat a friend. And who knows if your Indian people you will save?"

"OK. I'll put my 'power' at your disposal, but I don't know how it works!"

"Don't worry. At the appropriate time will know it happened to all of us".

So it was that Little Course was forced to intervene. He, however, did not know that the virus in me had acted in a particular way. If before, because of my insomnia, I was immune to attacks to force myself to sleep and dream, now I started to feel different. I don't know if the virus I did fall asleep, but what happened right after just seems a dream.

Since I could still move, I decided to try to do something. I began to wish that Incubus and the Brand he gets stuck. In fact, right after I saw that one fell to the ground and crashed. Their powers had moved or duplicated in me? I thought that Miss Backup obliged them to widen their controls against us. I tried to stop connecting with the baby, which finally calmed down. Nevertheless, I began to feel strange. The virus was having the upper hand. He was bringing me and my buddies toward certain death.

I decided to try to convince Miss Backup to send a final message in network extra-neural and extra-genetics that was created. Let resume Little Course to tell what happened.

Chapter XXXIV

I was brought around a room with three brick walls and lime and shatterproof glass. On the other hand, I see many women. There is also the Doctor.

"You start with her. She married Sheikh al-Jebel, and generates new genealogies. Their knowledge of genetics is too important to lose".

"It will never accept".

"We have convinced you. ... With good or bad, she will have to accept his new role. ... Then show you the next woman to be saved, because it becomes my Consort".

"Klein already has a wife, and a son!"

"It could not do anything for them".

I'm about to enter the room, when I seem to hear JLH whisper to me something. His voice, though, looks younger, like mixed with that of a child.

Once entered, I boot to the Doctor: "Oh, Inde! Stupidly I trusted Noor. Due to my now is forcing you to be evil to humanity".

"Don't worry. Now you will fare and use your powers as you will be asked".

"How are the others?"

"After that we will not treat you know him".

"Do you know how to treat myself? You're not a doctor".

"Then you have not yet noticed that I too have a non-standard DNA? My blood hides several surprises".

Now I do not know how, but I came spontaneously embrace it. In doing so, I felt like the heat go out from me.

Soon we find ourselves in the battlefield. I boot to friends, to allow everyone to heal. I start with Ornatrix, so that he can form a protective wall. Then I go from Heart-Sun, as requested by him. He immediately locks the men sent by Julius Caesar. Behind them, as in a Punic War, there is also a lookout, as leader.

After all, I ask healed Heart-Sun to try to block Julius Caesar for liberate Tempest. When I hug, I feel no sensation of heat, but a chilling cold. "Thank you, Little Course, you've saved me!" And then I hear thunder. Tempest is back!

At this point we've captured The Brand and Incubus, which will be locked up in prison for a long time, along with those acolytes here.

Now missing the call still four enemies. The Brand and Incubus have explained that their companions fled, to continue to melt the glaciers.

Chapter XXXV

In the world there are several glaciers, in the form of land or ice deserts, other mountain ranges: the Andes, the Alps, the Himalayas, Siberia, the two Poles, the Kilimanjaro.

These were the areas chosen by Sheikh al-Jebel to change the face of the Planet. Now the number seven requested Miss Backup became clear. Seven are the places that the worst tankers that this planet has ever had, he wanted to destroy. We had to divide — a place for each of us.

Probably also the four enemies were divided, leaving unattended three places. It wasn't easy to understand what the place to send anyone was. Since there was the uncertainty of who might be able to challenge anyone. Each of us maybe it was able to block oil refineries, but not everyone could fight. In particular, Little Course could only heal with a hug, while I, the writer of this report, I had lost my powers. The Doctor says that I can receive them temporarily from the others, but it's not entirely clear how. Maybe it's obligatory the presence of Miss Backup, or maybe not.

Anyway, here's how we divided us.

The Andes were Gilroy Bury and Miss Backup.

The Alps there was Little Course.

The Himalayas was assigned to JLH.

Siberia was assigned to the Doctor.

Heart-Sun went on the North Pole.

Tempest went to the South Pole.

Ornatrix was assigned to the Kilimanjaro.

Each area was particularly large, but the aim was to destroy oil refineries, before they melt the ice. Clearly, the mountain ranges are located inland, while the refineries often at sea.

In any case, to Gilroy Bury was not hard to find refineries by Sheikh al-Jebel. It was enough to go in the Neuquén province, home to the largest concentration of oilfields. This area lies to the East of the Andes, a strategic place to melt the glaciers. Flexing the time could easily overcome the guards. In her arms, she was holding her daughter. She could just disable the three refineries.

We supposed that the Alps and the Himalayas were secondary goals for our enemies; we sent us this Little Course and JLH.

For Little Course was easy. Discovered that had not been used in refineries, but a huge oil tanker docked in Trieste. This had to be detonated on the port of Trieste. The heat, due to a mixture of oil and hashish, he started a chain of disasters in the Alps, due to melting glaciers. Among the consequences there were earthquakes all along the path of the Apennines, coming up in Sicily, causing many casualties among the population or floods or the huge earthquake.

The major difficulty for him was to circumvent the surveillance. But he cleverly stepped triadic line. He began to sing with a series of "rain dances". The guards all stayed about the event. He then embraced each officer by sending a "genetic and anesthetic sleeping pill", which led to falling asleep suddenly. So he could come in and turn the boat. And deactivated the two dozen bombs scattered here and there. Then he went off without problems.

For JLH there was some difficulty in addition. The Himalaya is situated in an area that is politically dangerous. Also, there seems to be no place dangerous in countries touched by the Himalayan range. He hired an airplane to explore from above the Earth. Aircraft radio felt strange news: the water of the Taj Mahal has become slick! He decided to land at Agra Kheria. So he was able to recruit American military directly at the airport. Reached the Taj Mahal, his hypothesis was confirmed: the black liquid was oil-hashish of Sheikh al-Jebel. There were several men whose contact with this substance had caused changes to DNA. JLH believed not to himself. Had the same capacity to each of the enemies of tackle, but added! He defeated them with no problems. Now it was clear: the contact with oil allows JLH to acquire the powers of anyone who is near him.

In-depth investigations will be performed by Doctor later. But now let's get back to us because the Siberia (Сибирь) was not a walk. In fact, there was Sheikh al-Jebel, aka Noor al-'Iskenderun. The refineries were scattered throughout the Arctic Ocean. The Doctor used like never before his Genetic Scanner, shooting-flash, as he enjoyed telling his brother, against the enemy.

Four refineries were on the Kara Sea (Карское Море), on the Laptev Sea (море Лаптевых), and on the East Siberian Sea and the Chukchi Sea (Чукотское море). The last refinery was located on the Bering Sea, where was even Noor. Here the problems arose. When the Doctor attempted to intervene against Noor, is blocked. He was still in love with him, but realizes that it had to block his firm. The refinery had begun to explode. This would dissolve part of Siberia and Alaska, an area that had not been taken into account in the initial defense plan. Now the countdown had arrived almost at the end, missing a few seconds to the explosion that would have wiped out two lands on the planet, killing thousands of people. The Doctor seemed to have failed. However, if you think about what were the other three; we can understand that the danger was geographically spread!

In fact, Heart-Sun was not far away. On the North Pole she met Poliglottix. He was sure to win it without a care. The only North Pole refinery located at Lyon Seamount, Bering on the same line. Heart-Sun managed to block these refinery explosions and captured Poliglottix. Nevertheless, he had to leave immediately. He had received an SOS from his sister who was in the Bering Sea.

Meanwhile, Tempest had gone on the South Pole, the most difficult area of the Planet. Antarctica was full of refineries. Tempest was soon long to realize that many of these were merely feints. Serve only to mislead. In fact, there were only two, one near the Great Wall Station and the other near the Troll Station. They were supposed to explode later. In fact, the main objective was to recover all saved searches at the Amundsen-Scott South Pole Station.

There, Tempest found Glacier. The latter, although far from his Iceland, was at ease in a land of ice. He hadn't though given that Tempest had spotted her weak point. It was not easy to beat, but bringing Glacier inside the building, he was no longer able to defend itself, because the temperature was pretty high. Tempest was able to create a small storm inside the building, putting out Glacier, which surrendered to the authorities.

Ornatrix had reached the Kilimanjaro, where was Legend. The goal was not so much to blow up the oil, but to melt the glaciers of Africa's highest mountain via his three volcanoes, Kibo, Mawenzi, and Shira. Added a bit of mega-substance that Legend had brought with him, he would put on his knees much of Africa. Ornatrix risked her hair, creating a shield around the three craters. Indeed, Legend was alone, and his plan was to make it explode one by one, in order to send the volcano fluids in three directions previously designated. The project failed. And Legend was "bound" by Ornatrix and finally handed over to the authorities.

Maybe you'll wonder why anyone went to Iceland. Now, read the next two chapters to find out.

Chapter XXXVI

Bering Sea, meanwhile, thanks to its ability, Gilroy Bury comes when the battle is about to begin. At the same time, Tempest leverages its capabilities, making travel in the rest of the team, with the exception of JLH, not knowing that now even he is powerful.

When the others arrive, the Doctor is trying to fight against Noor, which takes advantage of its ability to combine his powers, trying to get stronger. When the others arrive, he decides to lead a strong earthquake, trying to unite his powers to those of others. The Earth starts moving. The ice begins to melt. Again, these seem to have been defeated.

Suddenly you hear a roar, followed by a very fast airplane. From here you throw someone, without a parachute. IS JLH! Is flying! When he lands, Noor understands that JLH has developed new genetic capacity. He decides to exploit them to create an even more powerful earthquake. The Doctor shouts: "JLH, go, or you'll be our ruin!"

JLH, instead, comes close. Tap the Doctor and Noor, acquiring the powers of both. At this point, he is able to combine his powers with those of others. So he genetically modifies Noor, who loses all power. The earthquake stops: the Planet is saved! Or better, for now it is safe. In fact, while the bad guys were stopped, still remains a question:

Chapter XXXVII

Why Iceland had been neglected? Because Iceland is a small island that has born Glacier. This island, for some time, was used for aerospace projects. She was very important for the project *Voyager Reverse*.

Recently, what looked like a meteoroid in progressing toward the Planet, proved a spacecraft from another planet. She bore the name "Earth".

We are on Planet Earth. April 19, 2010. Strange messages have reached astronomers of the Voyager Program. After careful consideration, they discover that Voyager 2 sent an encrypted message containing the coordinates that no telescope had ever identified before. These coordinates contained the name "Speculum".

From an in-depth study, it seems that the heliopause is a mirror to the Planet Earth, a sort of *parallel universe*, in which humans have different capabilities than the Terrans. Scientists are deciding what to do in order to communicate with this twin Planet.

Planet Speculum. Clínicas Universitarios y Psiquiátricos de Barcelona, Spain. Juan Pequeño Cuerno's enchanting the other patients, telling his last dream. A little over a month, every day, to his awakening, tells all her dreams. The thing that leaves open-mouthed is about characters whose names are identical to his, but translated into other languages, perform amazing acts.

Yesterday morning he told of how his namesakes had saved the world from a catastrophe. Today, says that he wants to travel with them to find out what it would be like to live in a "House Space".

Doctors are going crazy, trying to explain to other patients that it is just dreams dreamed up in bed, when the newscast is the announcement that a group of seven men and women plus a child has left for an intergalactic journey! What are their names? The same characters dreamed by Juan Pequeño Cuerno. What is the name of the project? It's called Voyager Ters.

Tables

The characters of the narrative

Character	*Heroic Name*	Nationality	Role	Powers
Mary Ivanovo	*The Doctor*	Russia	Geneticist	DNA recognition of others / Time trade / Can absorb the DNA of others
Joann Rajok	*Heart-Sun*	Presumably Russia	Data-processing technician	Pasting liquid / Infused mug / Absorption of heat energy (enlarged) or from rain (more control of force) / Acts in symbiosis with Tempest
Alexei			Friend of Joann Rajok	
Frederiqu e			Friend of Joann Rajok	
Alex Kids / Alexander Ivanovo		Russia	Father of Mary / War scientist	
Anne Petite		French	Mother of Mary	
Anne		Presumably	Pianist	Transmit

Ivanovo		Russia		nonstandard DNA to anyone
Alexander Ivanovo		Presumably Russia	Brother of Anne Ivanovo / Spy	
Peter Grant		Presumably Inghilterra	Doctor / Mary's uncle and husband of Anne	
Genna'ro The Brand		Presumably Italy	Professor of Genetics	Freeze time of bodies
J. H. Klein		Germany	Author of a book on Genetics	Weather control / Becomes Tempest
	Incubus		The Rector of University	Changing people's sleep
Vladimir Klein		Germany	Son of J. H.	Weather control / Becomes Tempest
	Tempest	Time	Exchange in time	Journey through time / Space navigation / Meteorological Control / Reinforces the power of Heart-Sun
W. A. Klein		Germany	Father of J. H. and grandfather of Vladimir / musician / ex surgeon	Weather control / Becomes Tempest
David Livingstone / Dottor	Legend	Tanzania (Lake Tanganyika	Descendant of David Livingstone and	Legge l'albero genetico delle persone

Livings		)	presumably of Ḥassan-i Ṣabb¬āḥ / Anthropologist / Promoter /	
John Little Horn	*JLH*	England	I	Insomnia (DNA standard) / Non-standard DNA to contact with oil
Leopoldin a Klein	*Wolfi (nickname)*	Germany	Mather of W. A. Klein	
H. G. Wells		London (England)	Scientist / Writer	
Ḥassan-i Ṣabb-āḥ	Old Man of the Mountain	Iran	Leader of Assassins	
Antonio Soli'nas	*Su Corru ("Il Corno") (nickname)*	Italy	Trader	
Sala'ris		Italy	Right arm Soli'nas	
Re		Italy	Ancestor of some characters	→
Charlema gne			King	
Gaius Julius Caesar		Rome	Dictator of Rom	
Brutus		Rome	Caesar's nephew	
Katia Kaiser	*Gilroy Bury*	Russia	Female student	Decipherer / Time adjustment / Can move in time and

				space the Doctor e Tempest
Moradh Lifneh	*Poliglottix*	Babel / Israel	Descendant of Sharkalisharri	Speak any language
Sharkalish arri		*Akkad*	Kingdom of Agade	
Flavia Orna	*Ornatrix*		Hairdresser	Can lengthen and harden his hair
Elisa Rajok	*Miss Backup*			Genetic Exchange / Can use and exchange DNA fractions
Noor al-'Iskandarū n	*Sheikh al-Jebel*		Oil Tankers	Remains forever young / Regerative power control / Hide its powers / Can combine his powers with those of other / Other powers undiscovered
Inde Diné	*Little Course*	The Navajo Texan		Care DNA with a hug
Dan Sky Manise	*Glacier*	Presumably Anglo-Icelandic		Changing the consistency of the ice

Locations

Site	Geographical location	Role	Facts
University		Almost the entire book	At least eighty percent of the book
Laboratory	University	Headquarters	At least eighty percent of the book
Grand Canyon	USA	The first experiments in the time of the exchange	Dramatic moments in history
Rail router		Solution	Rail crash
Tanzania	Africa	Legend	Investigative surveys
Lake Tanganyika	Tanzania		
Ruckwa	Tanzania		
Tanganikaland	Tanzania	Amusement Park	
Democratic Republic of the Congo	Africa		
Kigoma	Democratic Republic of the Congo		
London	England	Journey	Cameo by H. G.

		through time	Wells
Alamut (Alamut Castle)	Iran	Headquarters of the Assassins	
Bosa	Sardinia (Italy)	Dream of Heart-Sun	
Catalonia	Spain		Find a document
Babel	Babylon		Construction of the Tower
Israel		Patria of Poliglottix	
Agade	Akkad		
Church	Putifigari	Marriage	Has preserved an importnat document
South Eastern Anatolia	Turkey	Enemy base	Training base
Listasafn, Reykjavik	Iceland	Convention	Revelations on icebergs and glaciers
Port of San Diego	California	Docking of the Heart-Craft	Escape from the Grand Canyon
Andes	Argentine		Final batte
Alps	Europe		Final batte
Himalaya	Asia		Final batte
Siberia	Russia		Final batte
North Pole			Final batte
South Pole			Final batte
Kilimanjaro	Africa		Final batte
Bering Sea			Culmination

Tutors to Elisa

Personage	*Heroic name*	Materia
Maria Ivanov	The Doctor	Applied Sciences
Ioann Rajok	Heart-Sun	Computer Science
J. H. Klein		Mathematics
W. A. Klein		Music
John Little Horn	JLH	Literature
Katia Kaiser	Gilroy Bury	Biology and Chemistry
Flavia Orna	Ornatrix	Aesthetics